DAUGHTERS OF KHATON

DAUGHTERS OF KHATON

by

Merril Mushroom

LACE PUBLICATIONS

Library of Congress Cataloging-in-Publication Data

Mushroom, Merril, 1942–

    Daughters of Khaton.
    I. Title.
PS3563.U8353D3   1987   813'.54   87-29695
ISBN 0–917597–03–6

* * *

Printed in the United States of America.

First Edition.
First printing.

Cover design by Lambda Graphics, Denver
Cover illustration by Wendie O'Farrell

Lace Publications
POB 10037
Denver CO 80210-0037

An excerpt from this book appeared in a different form with the title Sisterworld in *Sinister Wisdom* #1, 1976.

ISBN 0-917597-03-6

to Mary

special thanks to Artemis, who knows
and to the Hylantree

PART ONE

1

"A fair-looking world!" cried Dennivan, peering at the scene on the scanner.

"Looks have been deceiving before," muttered Korith. His hand automatically stroked the plastic and metal beneath his trouser leg where flesh and bone once had been. During his last exploration, he had been bitten on the ankle by a tiny insect; and only through the swift skill of his partner's laser surgery was he able to return alive to the globe, although he left his rotting leg behind.

They watched the image on the screen, as the Explorer Globe Lycoperdon descended through the atmosphere. The two major land masses were connected at the north by a band of mountains and separated by two turquoise oceans which flowed together in a narrow neck at the southern pole. The larger continent was covered with blots of red, purple, and green, while the smaller continent was a kaleidoscope of gentle pastel tints.

The crew members of the Explorer Globe Lycoperdon were

weary. For decades they had lain in cold sleep, then roused to search among star systems for unpopulated planets that expanding humanity could safely colonize, returned to cold sleep for more decades, and awakened to search again. From among the planets they encountered, they screened out those which were promising for, yet uninhabited by, intelligent life. The Lycoperdon landed on eleven of these planets to further study them, and six of these new worlds proved possible to live on.

On each of these six planets, the doors of the Lycoperdon opened, and the crew went out from the globe to sample, study, and explore. They made discoveries, and some were not to their liking. On the second planet, the first crewman was killed while setting pikes into the face of an obsidian cliff. A sudden slide of jagged crystal boulders sliced, then crushed, then buried him. A man and a woman were lost on the third planet when their copter was snatched from the air by a gross creature that broke from a slime-covered sea over which they flew too low. On still another world, a crewman, over-confident in the apparent safety of an ordinary meadow, blundered into a stretch of soft and hungry swamp which seared his flesh from his bones even as it sucked him beneath the surface.

Reports were made and filed and relayed appropriately. The carefully calculated time allotted for the mission of the Explorer Globe Lycoperdon passed and began to approach completion. Once again the crew members were awakened from cold sleep. They turned their attention to the very last sector to be explored, while their thoughts continued to a point beyond these cycles to a time of rest and settling down in a home to first be found.

Now, the Explorer Globe Lycoperdon orbited the planet Khaton, searching for a landing site, a gleaming silver satellite among lilac and amber moons. As it slowly approached the surface, its great computer hummed and clicked, assimilating, sorting, and approving aspect after aspect of this new world. The six remaining crew members joined Captain Eliat in the control room, and the protective shields which covered the main viewport slid aside. Fourteen eyes watched as the globe hovered over a large open area on the smaller continent, then slowly descended until it touched the surface of the world and stopped.

"We'll key in the alerts, and then we can all get some rest," said

Captain Eliat. "In the morning we'll see what more the computer has for us and then send out a party to explore."

The crew members stood quietly for a while, looking out the viewport.

Robwill coughed. He was feeling young and vulnerable.

Lester muttered to himself.

Prechard kept her thoughts quiet. She was feeling very much The Only Woman On Board since Juna had been pulled down. Korith and Danal flanked her, one on each side, both hoping, as they always did, to rouse her interest in their maleness.

Darkness came gently outside the Lycoperdon, and moonlight tinted the distant shrubbery with changing patterns of lilac and amber. Little flying insects with big, soft wings fluttered against the viewscreen, until the protective shields slid to cover the huge window.

2

"All blessings, gentle flowers.
Blessings on your welcome fragrance.
Praises for your joyful colors.
May your fertile seeds be many,
Gentle sisters of the flower.
All blessings."

The voices of the singers faded away, and Amaranth stood tall before the mammoth Hylantree. The soft fabric of her festival robe shone against her skin, shimmering with the colors of the flowers which made up its weave. The Hylantree was very old. Its trunk was so thick that a dozen women holding hands could barely circle it. This mighty trunk branched into scores of limbs, and now, at the beginning of second season, thousands of flowers clustered in the huge green crown of leaves.

Amaranth stretched her arms out to the great tree. Her copper eyes shone. "Mother Hylantree," she rejoiced, "I, Amaranth, bring you greetings of love and celebration. All blessings, Mother, as we enter second season."

The limbs of the tree dipped and trembled, and a soft rustling sounded among the leaves. Singers raised their voices, and women moved forward to touch the ancient trunk. The tree quivered, showering sweet-scented petals over them. As the last woman brushed her hand over the smooth bark, a subtle thrumming swelled the air. Each person present bowed her head, and the message of the Mother gently penetrated deep within the soundless spheres of mind:

/Blessings to you, also, dear my children of the flesh. Rejoice with your sisters of the flower as we grow toward fruit and seed through second season. All blessings./ The Hylantree grew still, and a great joy permeated the souls of the women and burst from their lips in one mighty paean.

Amaranth turned, her face glowing, her eager eyes seeking, her colors—gold and copper—flashing in the light from the suns. Vitis ran toward her, violet eyes shining, the smoky mist of her robe blowing about her. She took Amaranth by the hands and spun her around. "My sister is more beautiful than the flowers she praises!" she cried.

"Her beauty is second to that of her friend," Amaranth replied softly. Then, suddenly, without warning, a foreign feeling of loneliness which she didn't understand descended over her and gripped her, plucking at her joy with sharp and greedy fingers. She pressed her fists against the fullness of her chest in an attempt to quell the peculiar surging of her heart.

"What?" Vitis' whisper was as soft as dusky fingers which she laid against Amaranth's golden cheek.

Amaranth placed her own hand over them, taking comfort. "I don't know." Her voice held traces of trepidation, and her next words followed slowly. "I have a feeling of something strange which I fear is coming toward us."

3

Dennivan suited up. It was his turn to work with the landside team. He tried not to think about the friends he had lost on past landwalks, but he could not obliterate the memories. Dominating his thoughts was the time Korith had been stung when they were teammates. He wished he could forget what it had been like when Korith's leg suddenly started to rot, putrescence spreading from the place on his ankle where the tiny bug had pierced him with its poison. He'd had to cut Korith free from the leg, working swiftly with his laser, while with all his heart and soul he reached out to his friend in comfort and support, wishing only that this were not happening.

That's the problem with cold sleep, he mused. *Not enough time passes between events for us to be able to work things through or else push them to the back of memory.*

Covered, at last, by protective jumpsuit, boots, and gloves, Dennivan went to meet with Danal and Lester in the vestibule where the landside team would receive final orders from Captain Eliat. Now, in spite of past tragedies, he was feeling excitement begin. He sensed no threat from this world but, rather, a strange attraction, a drawing of himself to this place, a feeling he had not before experienced on any of the other planets. He arrived at the vestibule and greeted Lester and Danal. He had worked with them both before. They were a good team. Dennivan flexed his fingers. He could hardly wait to leave the globe and get his hands on this new world.

At last Captain Eliat appeared. "The computer has no further information at this time," he said crisply. "It has found neither threat nor danger yet, but you men be careful and watch out for one another. We will, of course, monitor you at all times. I want all three of you back safe and sound." He clapped each of them on the shoulder, then stepped back into the main of the globe while Dennivan, Danal and Lester sealed themselves into the vestibule, opened the port, and exited.

Prechard monitored the screens with Korith. *Thanks be for cold sleep*, she thought, glancing at her teammate. *It keeps me from having to spend much time with such as himself.* She didn't mind teaming with Lester or Dennivan, and she loved working with Robwill; but she had a hard time with the overwhelming maleness that Korith and Danal projected. *At least this one isn't the lurker that the other one is*, she thought gratefully. Teaming with Korith was difficult, but teaming with Danal, especially alone, always gave her the creeps. And whenever she got the creeps she remembered the one on her home planet with whom she was matched, himself in cold sleep to await her return, so that they should begin their life together in the same time and at the same age. She felt her stomach begin to quiver with denial, and she turned her attention back to the viewscreen.

The transmitters were sending good, clear pictures. Danal and Dennivan were taking surface samples while Lester kept watch. Their protective coveralls were open only at the face and were covered there with a fine mesh screen. Tools and weapons swung from belts around their waists and across their chests. The collars and cuffs of their jumpsuits were fully equipped with complete contact sets to keep them linked with those aboard the globe.

Captain Eliat paced about between viewscreen and computer. *And what unsuspected threat hides here to get us?* he wondered. *This world appears to be as harmless as did the others. On them we had no warning, no cause to be suspicious; and four of my crew have perished. I have lost those for whom I am responsible. I am a Captain, and I am ashamed.*

He watched the images that the landing team transmitted back to the globe, listened to their sounds, and knew that even though he could call them if necessary, give orders to them directly if he needed to, that in the long run, should an emergency arise, he was powerless to save them. *I am a Captain*, he thought, *and, in fact, I am helpless.*

Suddenly a shrill shrieking noise sounded from the direction of the brush thicket that grew some distance away from where the landside team was working. The men looked up, startled, to see a huge flying thing rise from the shrubbery. It resembled a giant purple locust with long spines between its wings. It flew over the bushes in their direction, then crashed down, rose again, and flew away from them and out of sight.

"That was enormous!" said Dennivan shakily, laughing a little with nervousness. "I'm glad it decided to fly the other way, whatever it was."

"We got some good films to study," Captain Eliat's voice sounded in his ears from the speakers in the collar of his jumpsuit. "You men be careful. Use your weapons if you have to. I do not want another Incident."

Dennivan, Danal, and Lester returned to their work—clipping, sorting, sifting, classifying, and guarding. After a time, again in the distance, a wailing began. The men looked around. Dennivan shrugged. Danal shook his head. Lester grunted. The wailing continued. The men worked. Eventually, the wailing faded into silence.

4

Arum and Allium were a long way from home. They had caught a ride on a wild queequer, and it flew high and far with them before they were able to land it. Arum, as the eldest by two years, felt the most responsibility. True, Allium had done the urging, but she, Arum, had given in; and they had lassoed the shoulder spikes of the giant insect with their riding straps, throwing their loops over the horny protrusions which extended from the queequers back shell and pulling them tight.

As Arum and Allium settled themselves against their harnesses, the insect, startled by the sudden weight, whirred its multiplicity of strong wings and rose into the air.

"Queeee . . . querrrrrr . . ." it shrilled. "Queeeee . . . eeeeeee!" while the girls, laughing with the exhilaration of the ascent, dangled on either side of their mammoth steed.

But the queequer had just placed a parcel of eggs and was feeling light. It flew higher than the girls had ever gone, and by the time they could weigh their will on it heavily enough to bring it down, it had flown too far over a thicket to be able to find a place that was clear enough to land without breaking into the shrubs. At last the queequer was pressed into landing near a tiny pond, and Arum and Allium hastily loosed their riding straps.The queequer, finding the mildly oppressive weight gone, leaped explosively over the next several patches of shrubbery before it finally found a thick growth of the foliage in which it liked to nest. It folded its wings against its body and crept beneath the soft plants.

Arum and Allium looked about. There was very little clearing around the pond; they were closed in completely by the thicket. Allium turned to Arum. "We'll have to find a way back through the hedgings." She looked unhappily at the thicket over which they had flown.

Arum shrugged. "It'll be easy. You'll see. All we have to do is find a stream and follow the water." She pretended a nonchalance she did not feel. "Let's get a drink, first."

The two children bent to the pond to refresh themselves before starting on their trek through the brush. They were daughters of Amaranth, and they resembled her in their coloring. Arum's hair was pale apricot, the same shade as her soft eyes, and her skin was very fair. Allium's skin was darker, like flat copper, her eyes shone red-gold, and her fluffy hair was yellow. Both girls were wearing short, belted tunics that were dyed green, dark and pale, in four shades.

Arum rose, sighing. She rolled up her riding strap and hung it at her belt. Allium did the same, all the while casting distressed glances at the shrubbery. "Well," said Arum, "we may as well get started." She plunged into the thicket, followed closely by her sister.

The shrubs grew past the height of a tall woman, but they were thickest, often closely interwoven, only near the tops. A person of child size would travel with ease among the sparser maintrunks by bending below the top growth. Arum and Allium had often traveled through similar thickets nearer to their home, and now they bent slightly and scooted along beneath the nest of thin-leaved twigs, winding their way in and out among the trunks of the shrubbery until they were thoroughly lost. At last, Allium said hesitantly,

"We can't follow the water if we can't find a stream to begin with." Her voice squeaked, betraying her growing fear.

Arum stopped and turned to face her sister, trying to hide her own nervousness by replying in a reasonable tone, "Well, this thicket doesn't go on forever. We have to come out of it somewhere." She started off again, muttering under her breath.

Allium struggled after her, fighting back tears. She wasn't at all sure that Arum knew where she was going, and this thought caused a bubble of fear to form in her middle which made it difficult for her to stay bent over far enough to keep twigs from tangling in her hair. Sweat ran down her face and into her eyes, and she blundered against a pointed stone and cut her foot. Allium cried out at the sudden sharp pain. Then she sat down right where she was and began to wail loudly.

5

Wyoleth was pulling leatherleaf, which grew in small clearings among the thickets. She looked fondly at the plant beneath her hands. The pale green of new leaves shone from under the dark carapace of last year's growth. It was this old growth that Wyoleth was gently prying away, so that the new young plant would be free to grow. She carefully stored the old leaves in two large baskets which were made to fit over her shoulders.

Then Wyoleth heard a child crying and stopped her work. She wiped her hands on the hem of her tunic and rose, turning to determine from which direction the crying was coming. "Whatever is a child doing out here?" she said to herself, the slightest crease beginning on her brow. Then she smiled, as she recalled her own childhood not long past. "It's second season," she murmured. "The silly child probably flew a photh or a queequer too far and got lost." She chuckled as she bent down and crept into the thicket, moving toward the sound.

Arum was the first to hear movement in the thicket nearby. She stopped sniffling and looked at Allium. Allium stopped wailing, and a moment later, a woman crept through the shrubbery.

"Wyoleth!" cried the children and flung themselves upon her.

Wyoleth laughed and embraced the girls. "What kind of mischief have you been up to now?"

Arum and Allium glanced sheepishly at one another. "It was just this old queequer . . ." Allium muttered.

"Well, no matter," said Wyoleth. "Come with me. You can help me pull the rest of the leatherleaf, and then I'll take you home."

The three together returned to the clearing and set to work, and soon the baskets were filled with the tough, old growth, while every plant in the clearing reached newly freed leaves toward the suns.

Wyoleth stood up and adjusted the baskets comfortably against her back, then picked up her short, flat knife and sized priers and hung them at her side. She was wearing a plum-colored tunic with a bright blue belt. The skin of her face and her bare arms and legs glowed deep rose, and her eyes were violet. "You're really not too far from home at all," she told the girls. "We can cut across the edge of the Great Clearing, and then you'll see." They moved into the brush.

As they neared the Great Clearing, the shrubs began to thin out, and soon Wyoleth and the girls caught sight of a very peculiar happening — three strange people were in the clearing. One stood gazing about purposefully, while the other two seemed to be involved with a plant.

"That's a budaberry!" Allium exploded.

Arum giggled. "They're cutting it."

"Not everyone else does things the same way we do," Wyoleth reminded them, "but it is rather unusual. I wonder who they are, and why does that one," she pointed, "stare about so?" They watched the three strangers from the shelter of the thicket for a few moments. Then Wyoleth said, "How peculiar. I wonder what they are doing now. Let's go closer and find out."

6

Lester's heart gave a thud and his belly lurched as he suddenly realized that three slender forms had materialized from the high underbrush and were coming toward them. He called softly to alert the other men, then blinked, as he visually resolved the forms into the reality of women — no, one woman and two girl children. Dennivan remained kneeling, but his muscles tightened. Danal rose slowly to his feet. All three men watched the approaching figures carefully, and those monitoring the screens aboard the Lycoperdon were tense with alarm. They were not in any way prepared for this. Inhabited worlds were off-limits, and the computer was supposed to screen them out.

The woman strode toward Danal, Dennivan and Lester, the two girls moving behind her like green and golden reeds. They reminded Lester of stories he'd read about fairies of ancient times. When the woman reached the men, she stopped, looked them over carefully, then asked, "Why are you cutting the budaberry?"

The men stared, astonished, unable to answer, and the woman chuckled, "Will you not leave it for the tapple-withs?" She studied them, then continued in a more sober manner, "Who are you, strange sisters? Your fashion is unusual to me. You are rather thick-set, I would say, and your dress is peculiar; but no doubt you are sisters of the flesh. I am Wyoleth, and I am curious to know why you hide your faces." Etiquette prevented her from phrasing this last as a direct question. She pointed at the distant globe. "Is that your pod? From which sister of the flowers comes a pod like that? And at second season? I have never known a pod to fly at second season!"

Dennivan was the team's anthropologist and expert on cultures. Now, he pushed aside his face veil in order to reveal that he was not threatening. "I am Dennivan." He fell easily into the dialect. "With me are Danal and Lester." He gestured for the other men to show their faces. "We are from the Explorer Globe Lycoperdon which you see beyond us. And you?" For a moment he dared to hope that perhaps this woman and these girls were from another explorer mission that had somehow happened to cross theirs. That would explain both their presence and their common language.

"I am Wyoleth," she repeated. "Sisters, I would know more about you. Will you come with me to meet with Amaranth?"

Dennivan felt a chill go through his belly at the invitation. Something, he felt, was not quite right about all of this, but he couldn't put his finger on exactly what it was. "Well," he began, stalling, his thoughts racing, "I must consult with my companions."

Wyoleth nodded at the girls, and the three of them withdrew to a discreet distance, leaving the men privacy to talk.

"Well, I'll be . . ." Lester muttered.

"This is a bad situation," Dennivan interrupted him. "We have to get away from here."

"You men!" Captain Eliat's voice sounded from the receivers in their collars. "You go with her!"

"What do you mean?" Dennivan whispered into his own collar transmitter. "We can't do that. We are caught here in error."

"Yes," agreed the captain. "The Mistake has been made, and we will find and repair the cause of it; but for now I say go with her. We must learn what we can of this alien culture."

"Don't look too alien to me," Danal snickered. "That one's a doll." He glanced over at Wyoleth.

"I don't feel right about this, Captain," Lester broke in. "We are not supposed to be here. I think we should leave."

"No," said the captain. "We are here now, and the damage has been done. We may as well salvage what we can. The computer has not indicated any potential threat on this world. You must go with this woman and meet with her leader."

"I don't know, Captain . . ." Dennivan began.

"Are you questioning my orders, Dennivan?" The Captain's tone was ominous.

"Oh, no, sir. No, sir. I was just stating an opinion."

"Well, Dennivan, you have every right to your opinion, as long as you follow Orders. Now, you men go on with these people. Don't worry. We'll keep you carefully monitored."

Big deal, Lester thought resentfully, as though monitoring us would be of any use or help us in the case of actual danger. But he could not argue with the captain's orders.

Dennivan dared to hesitate no longer. He stepped towards Wyoleth and the girls, smiling. "We would be honored to join you." His face felt as though he were wearing a plaster mask.

Wyoleth nodded her head. "Then follow." She turned and walked back into the thicket, the girls behind her.

Danal, Lester and Dennivan stared desperately at one another, all fighting their panic. "Go!" sounded the captain's voice at the necks, and they went.

7

The men had to bend nearly double to clear the thick brush above the widely-spaced trunks. Wyoleth glanced back at them and laughed. "The tallest women don't often travel through the thickets, it's much too uncomfortable; but there is no other way to go from here. We won't be in it very long." She moved easily among the trunks, bending at her neck, waist, and knees, and Lester, Danal, and Dennivan tried to copy her posture as they followed her. Lester's muscles ached. His legs were strained from this unaccustomed position of his body, and whenever he tried to ease himself, he would plow into the tight nest of twigs overhead. He wondered how long "not very" was, and he hoped grimly that the crew members aboard the globe were able to accurately keep track of himself and the other two men. He reminded himself that he must maintain trust in his captain, that Captain Eliat would not make decisions that would put any of them in danger. He should have more faith in the captain's judgment. Lester rubbed the back of his neck. They had been pushing through this tangle for a very long time. He glanced at the smaller child who was moving among the trunks to his left. She showed no sign of any discomfort, and she kept staring at him, hardly took her eyes off him. Lester's scalp prickled, and he quickly looked away from her. The other child was up ahead to the right of Danal and Dennivan who followed close after the woman. Lester felt almost as though they were being herded. Trusting his captain was becoming more difficult for him by the moment.

Sweat poured from Lester's face and settled into his collar, adding to his misery. His nose began to run, and he had no handkerchief. The little light that filtered through the branches seemed to be dimming, and Lester had an uncomfortable feeling of being trapped in this thicket after dark, at the mercy of all and anything, too exhausted to be able to defend himself, his comrades unable to reach him. He wondered morbidly if his friends aboard the globe would be attacked too. Perhaps he, Danal, and Dennivan should break free of these people and return to the globe while there was still time, while they were still able to. If necessary, the three of them could throttle a woman and two girl children, but what if their men showed up before they could get away? Lester sniffled and worried, moving onward, wishing he could talk to his crewmates without the girls and woman overhearing.

They came to a tiny brook that wove through the brush, and Wyoleth turned to parallel it. The girls cried out and ran ahead. Then the shrubs began to thin, and soon, Danal, Lester, and Dennivan followed the woman out of the thicket and into the muted light of late afternoon.

8

Arum and Allium suddenly recognized where they were when they saw the brook. They looked at one another, then ran ahead, shouting excitedly. As they broke from the thicket, they moved close together to more easily discuss the strange happenings.

"I never saw anyone who looks like that," Arum gasped, as the girls sprinted across the field and onto the path that led through the woods.

"Me neither," Allium replied between breaths. "Do you think maybe they are from the forests?"

"I don't know. Maybe. But in a pod? And at second season?"

As they ran past the toola patch, they saw Pahma and Ganvyla who were working between the rows. The girls skidded to a stop. "Greetings, grown ones," called Arum breathlessly.

Tall, fat Pahma stopped digging and leaned on her hoe. "Greetings, sprouts," she replied. "What passes?" She ran her fingers through her short fluff of white hair, pushing it back from her forehead where the perspiration beaded on mahogany skin.

"We were riding a queequer," Allium said, words tumbling rapidly from her mouth in her excitement. "We got lost, and Wyoleth found us, and then we found three . . ." she paused for breath.

". . . very strange sisters," Arum completed the sentence. "They were cutting a budaberry," she said in a confidential tone, as though to confirm the fact of their strangeness.

Ganvyla came over to stand beside her friend. She was wiry, with green eyes, olive skin, and thin, sharp features. "So where are you going now, younger ones?"

Arum and Allium looked at one another. "I guess we had better tell Amaranth, don't you think?" asked Allium.

Arum nodded. "She'd want to know they are coming before Wyoleth gets there with them."

"You'd best be off then," Pahma agreed, blue eyes shining in the darkness of her face. "Later, then." She waved as the girls ran off. Then she and Ganvyla returned to their work.

"Later, again," called Arum, as she and her sister sprinted down the path.

They rounded the curve which led to their home, slipped past the hanging mosses and into the main chambers that were walled with woven fabrics stretched among a planting of banyangs. The chambers were empty. "C'mon," Arum whispered urgently, and she led her sister around a spreading, palmlike bush and onto a stone walkway. "There she is!"

Amaranth was sitting on an elaborately carved stone bench under an arbor of pink and purple bellflowers. Next to her sat Amanita the priest, while Vitis paced about nervously behind them. Amanita had arrived moments earlier with the simple message, "Amaranth, something comes here," and the words echoed through the caverns of Amaranth's recent memory, bringing a return of her dream feeling of confusion. She stood up and addressed the priest, "I must speak with the Hylantree. I need an oracle."

Amanita nodded. "We can consult with The Mother after dark."

"But now," Amaranth began, then stopped as she saw her daughters running towards her.

"Wyoleth's coming," gasped Allium.

"With three *very* strange," Arum puffed.

"Sisters!" sputtered Allium.

9

Sighing with relief, the three men stood straight, arched their backs, and shook the cramps out of their legs. The brook they followed had grown wider and deeper, and now it broke apart into a series of tiny rills which became lost in the field that lay before them. The grass was thick with clumps of flowers of such intense shades of orange and pink that looking at them dazzled the eyes of the men. Bordering the field was an arc of trees with slender, grey trunks atop which rose a high tower of chartreuse leaves jeweled with deep red and purple flowers. The trees ended at a line of small hills, and above these mounds, the three suns setting shone dimly, ringed by concentric circles of lilac and amber mist.

As the men followed Wyoleth across the field, a heavy perfume drifted to them from the flowers, and Lester felt his throat constrict, as his memory thrust at him an old legend wherein the heroine and her three companions were overcome into unconsciousness while crossing a field of flowers. He was relieved when they reached the trees, and Wyoleth led them along a path into the woods.

After some distance, the path forked, and Wyoleth swung down a smaller trail, then pushed aside a hanging curtain of grey moss and held it for the men to pass. They stepped by Wyoleth and stopped. Before them, a structure of iridescent fabric was interwoven among the trunks and branches of several small trees to form an intricate series of chambers. The men started forward, then stopped again so short that they bumped together, as a woman appeared out of the forest before them. She was larger than any of the men, and she carried herself with great power and dignity. Her sleeveless robe of soft green material reached the tops of her bare feet. Her bright yellow hair was twisted through with flowers, and her copper-colored eyes flashed as she studied the men for a moment, then held golden arms out to them and said softly, "I, Amaranth, greet you with ceremony and bid you welcome."

10

"Will you step into my parlor?" invited Amaranth, and Dennivan mentally completed an ancient rhyme: said the spider to the fly. He looked at Lester who also knew the verse. Lester's cheeks were red, and he was sweating. The skin at the corners of his mouth was pale green.

The stately woman drew them after her. They passed through the maze of trees and down a walkway made from flat, gay-colored stones that had been pressed into the earth. To their left, a rockery towered, overgrown with delicate vines and ferns. A spring of water trickled among the plants, hung and fell from jutting rocks, and splashed into the pool beneath from a score of diminutive cataracts. Past the pool, the path led to a cluster of arbors that were cleverly laced together with their own diversity of vines and linked by stone benches and archways which were worked into ornate designs.

Amaranth motioned for the men to sit down. Then she lifted from the stone table next to her a goblet filled with green, sparkling liquid. She sipped from the goblet, then held it out to Dennivan.

Dennivan sipped. The drink was cool and minty, and it eased his parched throat. Silently he held the goblet out to Lester, continuing the ritual.

Here it comes, thought Lester. The drug or the poison. He took the goblet and raised it to his lips, but he only pretended to drink. To his embarrassment, his stomach gave a loud rumble.

Amaranth looked at him and chuckled. After Danal had taken his drink, she said, "The meal is ready. We can go and eat."

Lester gagged on fantasies of poison. He coughed to cover it. His throat was sticking together, and he had to force the words out: "Oh, no, that's all right. I . . . my stomach does that. It doesn't mean a thing. I'm not really hungry. I'll eat later, back at the globe."

"You may eat when you wish," Amaranth said. "I will eat now. Would you join me?" she asked Dennivan and Danal.

"Thank you. We would be pleased to," Dennivan responded for them both. He glared at Lester, eyes hard and commanding, and Lester followed as they left the chambers, a chill of helplessness flooding from his belly through his limbs.

Amaranth took the men down a narrow path away from the arbors. "Perhaps, strange sisters," she said as they walked, "you would tell me about yourselves while we eat. I must offer apologies in advance should we deviate from any custom you might have that differs from those which we keep. We will do our best to make you comfortable until tomorrow when you can return to your pod."

Tomorrow? Lester tripped and fell flat on the ground.

"I appreciate your hospitality, lady," said Dennivan, ignoring Lester who climbed to his feet and trotted to catch up with them.

They reached a clearing that was circled by huge trees with wide, branching leaves which formed a canopy over part of the area. At the other side of the clearing, a fire burned in a stone pit, and over the fire hung an enormous kettle which puffed steam from a long, thin spout. Scores of women and girls jostled each other around two long wooden tables set to either side of the fire. On the tables were polished wooden plates, sticks, and platters piled with food.

Amaranth gestured for each man to take a plate and a stick. The sticks were tapered at one end into two tines, while the other end had been carved into a small bowl. Amaranth's fingers fluttered among the platters on the table, and she deftly placed morsels of food on the plates which the men held.

The food was so tasty that Lester was unable to choke on it or even to gag. There were several kinds of raw, pale green shoots — some sweet and cool, while others had a pungent flavor or a subtle bite. All were crisp and juicy. There were tiny seeded rolls with sweet syrup, a smooth paste that resembled a nut butter, and tender leaves with an acid flavor rolled around a spicy filling and served hot with sauce.

"So," said Amaranth, when they had seated themselves on the ground at the edge of the clearing, "tell me about yourselves, who you are and where you are from."

Dennivan hesitated. Above all, he wanted to be careful of appearing godlike to these apparently primitive people. "My name is Dennivan," he responded, "and my companions are Danal and Lester." He indicated each in turn. "We are on a mission of exploration in the service of the United Planetary Researchers." He waited to see what reaction she would have to these words.

His speech seemed to hold no great significance for Amaranth. "Are you, then, not of Khaton?" she asked cooly.

"We are not of Khaton," Dennivan confirmed.

"The pod," Amaranth continued, "flies at second season?"

"The pod flies at all seasons."

"Then where is your home?"

"The pod is our home."

"How strange," mused Amaranth. Then she rose. "But I must now attend to other matters of importance. Have a pleasant guesting, sisters. Vitis will show you your chamber, and I will see you in the morning."

11

The men looked around. Women and children sat in small groups, eating. Many of them cast curious glances at the men, and a few smiled at them, but no one made any attempt to approach them or to speak to them. There were no other men besides themselves, and Lester felt the hair on his neck rise and his scalp prickle, as he realized that, in fact, he had seen no men since they arrived at this village. Daylight was almost gone, and scores of lanterns were lit in the clearing. In the muted light, the men saw a woman approaching. Her skin was dark as her hair, and she wore a robe of filmy stuff that revealed the movements of her body against the light. The men stood up.

"Pleasant evening, strangers," said the woman. "I am Vitis. Would you eat more?"

The men looked at their empty plates, then at one another. "I think we have eaten enough, thank you," Dennivan answered.

"Good. Come, then." She led them across the clearing, motioning for the men to set their soiled dishes on one of the tables as they passed. Then they were in the forest, moving among tall plants and between tentlike partitions, until they finally stopped before a flap that hung between two rough-barked trees. Vitis bent and lifted a corner of the flap. "Your chamber." She motioned for the men to enter, then followed them under the flap.

The men hummed with surprise. They stood in a large room with walls of opaque fabric and a thick roof of living leaves. In the center of the room was a low table of carved wood upon which burned three lanterns of the same type that lit the clearing. Around the table were laid three pallets of soft moss covered with lengths of thick, nappy fabric.

"Here," Vitis led the men over to a depression in the corner of the room. A low stone well with a wooden cover was set in the center of the depression, and over it a thick vine was supported by a series of wooden stocks. She pulled one end of the vine free, and a stream of water trickled from it and ran down the slope of the floor to drain away at the base of the stone wall. "This is for drinking and washing," she explained, as she hung the vine back up, "and here," she removed the cover from the circle of stones and looked significantly at the men. A hole went down into the ground — a shaft leading into darkness far below — from which came an earthy aroma. "I must apologize," Vitis continued, "for the rudeness of your chamber. We had not much time to prepare."

The men were tired. They murmured appropriate phrases of appreciation and all cast longing glances at the pallets. "Have a restful night," Vitis said. "I will see you in the morning," and she slipped out beneath the flap.

12

Amaranth and Amanita crouched over a brazier of burning herbs, facing one another. Their eyes were closed, and they swayed slightly from side to side, as they inhaled the fragrant smoke. Amaranth began to chant, slowly, softly, "Oh, Hylantree, Hylantree, Mother of us all, help me to find within myself the seed of the many-petaled flower which grows ever toward her reflection in the light and the darkness of pure truth. Lend me this night the staff of your wisdom to help me find my way. Aid me, Mother, in my need, my confusion, and my fear."

Smoke billowed from the brazier, almost hiding the forms of the two women, as swiftly, in reply, they felt the presence of The Mother. / What troubles my child of the flesh? /

Amaranth answered wordlessly, / Tell me, Mother of these strange sisters. Advise me of the best course of action to follow. My soul has been disrupted by their arrival. /

The Mother responded with no hesitation: / They are sisters and yet not sisters, although they assuredly are of the flesh. Their pod is a pod but not of the flowers. It carries the strangers of the flesh, but it bears no new life of root and leaf.This have I found of them: / Images flowed from the essence of The Mother to priest and Amaranth. All that pervasive intelligence had been able to glean from the crew since their arrival became known to the women – the camaraderie of people involved together in exclusive situations, the darkness of space and of cold sleep, the urge to expand, and the need to conquer. Feelings flooded through Amaranth and Amanita that were like their own but not their own – discovery, loss, joy, pain, hope, fear, doubt, greed, wonder, expectation; and behind it all was a constant lonely longing, an unrecognized separation from the totality of spirit, and an unconscious need to trust and to become whole again. This was the sum of the strangers as received and relayed by the Hylantree, and Amaranth recognized that this was, indeed, the source of her uneasiness.

/What must we do, Mother?/ Amaranth pleaded silently.

/ You must learn of one another, dear my children / replied The Mother. The message ended, The Mother departed, and Amaranth felt the world around her pressing in on her senses.

Amanita took her firmly by the hand. The ruby eyes of the priest glowed like fiery pits in the light of the amber moon. "So we must," she whispered, "and so we will."

13

Dennivan, Danal and Lester lay on their moss beds, heads pillowed on their arms and collars pulled up over their ears. They spoke together quietly, discussing the situation with each other and with the crew aboard the globe. Dennivan had just completed a taped report spoken softly into the tiny transmitter in his sleeve.

"We have some really fine pictures," Prechard's voice came from the receivers in the collars of the men. "That big purple bug was something, eh? Seems to be harmless, though, as far as we've been able to determine."

"Yeah," grunted Lester. "Now what about these people? We are sort of stuck here, and I could use some reassurance about our safety."

"Looks to me like you've fallen right into the middle of heaven," Korith snickered. "The only thing missing is one of those dolls in your bed."

"Shut up, Korith," Prechard interrupted, offended.

"Be serious," spoke Dennivan. "Can we be sure that in back of all this hospitality there isn't a real threat? You guys are sitting up there watching it all, but we are right in the middle of it."

"So far, we have seen neither evidence nor indication of any danger to you," said Captain Eliat. "This is a most unusual situation, and I am not sure how it happened; but we must take advantage of it to learn as much as we can. Now, since I am responsible for your welfare, and since I cannot guarantee that you are entirely safe and secure, I expect you to post watches through the night and continue to be careful. I commend your behavior so far. I will keep you monitored from here at all times— I do not want to have another Incident."

"The thing that bothers me," continued Danal, "is where are the men? I mean, we haven't seen another man yet."

"Maybe they're busy with hunting or whatever the men do," said Korith. "Maybe you'll see them tomorrow."

"Yeah, maybe they're all locked in cages or being fattened in dungeons, too," Lester grumbled.

"You've been reading too many legends," Dennivan retorted. "Go to sleep. I'll take the first watch, and then I'll wake Danal, and maybe by the time he wakes you, you'll be in a better frame of mind. You guys back there take care, too. Mind your alerts."

"Yeah," Lester threw one parting shot, "maybe the men are on their way to get you."

14

In spite of their nervousness, Danal, Lester and Dennivan all
slept soundly when their turns came. As the triple suns rose, the
first light of morning illuminated the woven walls of the chamber,
causing them to become translucent, and a warm, pink glow lit the
interior.

Danal was on watch when the curtain at the doorway was lifted
and Vitis entered. "Good morning, Danal." At the sound of her
voice, the other two men came instantly awake. "I trust you all slept
well."

"We slept well, Vitis, thank you," Danal replied, finding her
name suddenly sweet upon his tongue.

She smiled at him, her teeth flashing white behind her full lips
and just the tip of her pink tongue showing. She held his brown
eyes with the gaze of her violet ones for an instant, and Danal felt
himself flush. Then she stepped to a corner of the room and released a section of the fabric which made up the wall. A stream of
sunlight flooded into the chamber.

"Amaranth would like for you to take breakfast with her," Vitis
said to the men. "I will wait for you outside." She slipped beneath
the door flap.

Danal stared after her, and Lester guffawed, "You look smitten,
my friend."

Danal closed his mouth and swallowed hard. Lester and Dennivan rose from their pallets, and the men washed and straightened
themselves. They ducked out the door and found Vitis waiting. She
led them through another series of chambers and into a small court-
yard framed by flowering hedges.

Amaranth sat in a large, basket-like chair. "Good morning,
strangers," she said.

The men sat down on the ground. A very thin woman with ruby-
red eyes, pink hair, and startlingly white skin was sitting next to
Amaranth. Amaranth gestured toward her. "Amanita is priest," she
said to the men. Amanita nodded curtly, and the men nodded back.

Nearby, Amaranth's two daughters stood side by side, staring at the men with wide eyes.

Then, two older girls appeared carrying trays laden with cups, a pitcher of steaming liquid, and a platter of small cakes. The women and girls served themselves, and, as no one waited on them, the men followed their example. The cakes were soft and warm, fresh and filled with sweet, chewy bits. The drink was hot, bitter, and undoubtedly a stimulant.

At length, Dennivan looked over at Amaranth and broke the silence. "You have been most kind and gracious, lady, but one thing has continued to puzzle me."

Amaranth put down her cup. "Speak, Dennivan, and I will answer if I can."

"Well," he ventured, then asked hastily, before he lost his nerve, "Why do you keep us among the women? Where are the men?"

"Men?" Amaranth looked directly into his eyes. "What are 'men'?"

Danal choked on his cake, while Lester inadvertently swallowed a huge gulp of his drink, nearly scalding his throat. Dennivan's face twitched, and he shook his head. "You've got to be kidding!" he blurted. Then he continued more rationally, "Surely, lady, you have men in your tribe. Males? Fathers? Perhaps you use a different name for them."

Amaranth shook her head. "I am sorry, strange sister, but I do not know of what you speak."

"Look," Dennivan tried again, "you are all women," he motioned toward the seven of them, "and we are men," he indicated the three of themselves.

Amaranth shrugged. "We are all sisters of the flesh," she reasoned. "Perhaps you are asking for other strangers. In that case, the only 'men' we know now or ever have known are yourselves and those inside your pod who wait for you."

Dennivan stared sharply at her, wondering how she had known about the others aboard the globe, but she was speaking again: "Robielde will take you back to your pod now. Bid your sisters there to return with yourselves to us. We must learn of one another. This The Mother has said." She rose, then, and without another word, without so much as looking at the men, she walked from the clearing.

Amanita leaned forward, her eyes shining in her face like blood upon snow. "So, you are truly from another world, eh?" she addressed Dennivan.

"What do you know of other worlds?" he countered.

"We know that there *are* other worlds, of course, but *of* them we know not. You may enlighten us, but all in good time. It will be of greater value for us to learn of one another when you return with your sisters from the pod."

15

Robielde was a diminutive woman with soft, plum-colored skin, dark green eyes, and brown hair which she wore in two coils over her ears. As she led the men back through the thicket, she chattered amiably. "Your pod must be very different to fly at second season. On Khaton, second season is of the flowers. They grow through fruit to seed, and only at the end of fourth season do the pods begin to fly."

The trip through the thicket didn't seem so long and tedious now that the men were returning. They moved faster, and soon, with a rush of relief, they arrived at the clearing where the globe rested. "Your shining pod is certainly a great and massive one!" Robielde observed.

Dennivan edged closer to Danal. "When we get aboard," he muttered out of the corner of his mouth, "you take her to see quarters so that the rest of us can have a little private discussion. Better yet, get Prechard to take her around." He winked at the other man.

As they climbed through the globe's open entrance, Danal took Robielde by the arm and steered her past the men who waited inside. "These are Korith, Robwill," he pointed to each of them in turn, "Captain Eliat, and this is Prechard. Here, she'll show you around the globe." He thrust Robielde toward Prechard, annoyed at almost being excluded and left with the woman.

"So," said Captain Eliat, as soon as the women were out of sight, "the Accident has happened. The planet is populated, and the computer missed this fact on its first analysis. We have landed directly among the People here, and now we have no chance to sneak away. Now we are obligated to Handle the Situation."

"Well," interjected Korith, "the 'Situation' so far does not seem to be in the least unpleasant, if you know what I mean."

"Not funny, Korith," the captain reproached him. "Primitive populations tend to deify planetary explorers. We must have a care for this."

Lester was shaking his head. "I just don't like it. I don't like any of it at all. Where are the men, anyhow? What is all this 'what are men?' crap? I think we had better watch out. There may be some very unpleasant surprises in store for us. And if these women are, as it appears, the force in power on this world, we may need Prechard to act as a sort of diplomat or go-between for us."

"I remember old legends," Robwill added, "about a race of women who trapped men to breed with them, then killed the men and ate them. They also ate the male babies . . ."

"Nonsense, Robwill! Stop panic-mongering!" commanded the Captain. "It is no joking matter. The great computer has studied the situation and has advised us. It has recognized, located, and corrected the cause of the original error. These people appear to be an isolated colony of some sort. They seem altogether innocent, harmless, even childish. The computer has advised that we take advantage of the situation and study these people. It has instructed that we send the globe into controlled orbit with myself holding the call unit. It has advised that we go among these people and meet with the men in charge to find out where they are from and how they came to be on this world. However, I will not force anyone to leave the globe who might be afraid."

Dennivan coughed.

Robwill cleared his throat.

Lester shuffled his feet.

Voices sounded from the long corridor—Prechard speaking loudly to give warning of their arrival. Then Robielde appeared in the doorway, Prechard following. "Truly you have an unusual pod, sisters," she remarked. "It is unlike any I have ever seen. Now, shall we return for your guesting?" She smiled at Prechard, and Prechard suddenly felt embarrassed in front of her crewmates.

Captain Eliat stepped up to replace Prechard, escorted Robielde out the door, ignoring the others and leaving them to make their own decisions as to what they would do. They all followed silently, and the great door slid slowly closed behind them. Captain Eliat pressed a stud at his belt, and the Lycoperdon lifted silently through the air to orbit around the planet Khaton.

"What passes with your pod?" asked Robielde.

"It must return for a while," answered the captain, "to its place in the sky."

"Its place in the sky," mused the woman. "Truly, strange sisters, we have much to learn of each other."

PART TWO

1

Lester awoke suddenly. His eyelids stuck together, and he rubbed away the crust, scratching into the corners with his fingernails. Behind his eyes, a dull drumming began to spread ripples of ache through his skull. He was overwhelmed by a feeling of confusion. Pulling up onto one elbow, he struggled to orient himself. He was lying on a mat which rested on a floor of earth carpeted with soft mosses. One corner of the delicate fabric that made up the walls of his chamber was raised, revealing a little clearing ringed by trees and brush, among which were woven the chambers which housed Lester's companions.

Lester rolled to his feet, splashed water on his face, ducked under the corner flap, and stood in the clearing looking about. Soon Dennivan emerged from his own chamber nearby. "Hi," he called.

"Hi," Lester replied. They looked at each other uncertain of what to do next. Then, one by one, their companions came out of their respective chambers and into the clearing.

"Well," said Korith, breaking silence, "what now?"

Prechard cleared her throat. "I could do with some eat-and-drink."

"Hungry," Lester agreed.

They milled about aimlessly, feet beating the ground to go but stopped for lack of direction. "What do you think, Captain?" Danal questioned, craving to be told what to do next, "do we wait around, or do we go exploring?"

"Greetings, strange sisters." As though she had heard the question, Allium entered the clearing. "Come with me." She motioned toward a path. Tentatively, the crew members followed her through a mass of soft, clinging vines and onto the bank of a pond. Great clusters of puff-fungi grew on the grassy rise, and among these were seated Amaranth, Amanita, Vitis, and Arum.

Allium stopped before a giant labyal which grew among the fungi. She folded back the petals. The stamens of the flower were thick and bore large globes of pollen, while a pool of moisture glistened in the shallow calyx. Carefully, Allium plucked off pollen globes and handed them to the men. Then she dipped some of the heavy liquid from the heart of the labyal into small cups and distributed them all around.

Danal bit into the ball of pollen and was surprised to find that it was moist and sweet, tasting something like the custardy rolls which he remembered from his childhood. The nectar was thick and cool and left a fresh feeling inside the mouth. Danal devoured three pollen rolls and then sat back, belched, and patted his stomach.

"Fair morning, gentle sisters." Wyoleth trotted down the bank toward them. "I need three helpers to transport the fresh leatherleaf to the turners. Would any of you care to go, strange sisters?"

Danal stood up, speaking before his thought was completely formed. "I would go, Wyoleth."

"And I," Robwill followed.

"And I," Prechard joined them.

"Come, then," Wyoleth said to the three, "and we will get the baskets; and then we can be on our way."

As the four of them left the clearing, Lester wiped the back of his hand across his mouth and looked at Amanita who was staring at him. He felt tension flow between them like a heavy cable linking them together, and he leaned forward, frowning, feeling the need to break contact. "So, priest," his voice sounded loudly, "tell me, then, what is your function?"

Amanita's eyes narrowed for the merest flicker of a moment. "My function, Lester?" She tossed his challenge back to him, "Would you meet with the Hylantree in order to discover for yourself? Would you have a small part in the ceremony of our people?"

A chill swept through Lester, as his imagination presented him with a sudden and graphic fantasy of torture and male sacrifice. Carefully, he replied, attempting to turn the conversation back to her. "How came you to be priest?"

"I am priest. Such is my function." She turned away from Lester, and he felt the tension release, then disappear.

Korith and Dennivan stood up, and Korith turned to the captain. "We're going to roam around for a while, Captain. We'll be back in touch."

As the two men left the clearing, Amaranth turned to Lester and Captain Eliat. "Now I need to go to the place of the tapple-withs. Would you join me?"

"I would be pleased to," answered Captain Eliat.

"And I," agree Lester, against his better judgment but not to be left alone.

2

Danal, Robwill, and Prechard followed Wyoleth through a clump of tall arch reeds and into a large space where a group of women worked among piles of raw leatherleaf, soaking, stretching, and scraping the material. An ebony-skinned woman stepped forward, silver eyes twinkling. "I see you brought a fine, large lot," she laughed, indicating the baskets slung over the shoulders of the four people.

"Pull it loose for us, would you, Camas?" Wyoleth asked.

Camas unloaded the leatherleaf and stacked it on the ground, then helped Wyoleth, Prechard, Robwill, and Danal to unfasten and remove the baskets. "Now," she said, "let's put this in to soak." She picked up an armload of the fresh leatherleaf, carried it over to a deep trough that was filled with a milky-looking fluid, and slipped one section at a time into the liquid.

Prechard and Robwill were working with Camas pressing the wet leaf with wooden paddles, and Danal was helping Wyoleth peg a piece down on a stretcher, when Vitis entered the clearing. "Many greetings," she said cheerfully.

The women returned greetings, not pausing in their work, but Danal could not take his gaze from Vitis, and his hand at the stretcher slowed. She walked over to where he was working. "So, tell me, strange sister, is your work pleasing to you?" Danal nodded. His throat felt swollen, and he was unable to speak. Vitis smiled, and a million butterflies fluttered in Danal's belly. "Later, then," she said, and slipped away through the archreeds.

Prechard turned to Camas. "Everyone I have observed here so far," she said, "seems to be content with whatever she is doing. By what means do you decide which tasks fall to whom?"

Camas looked up, silver eyes shining in the night of her face. "Each does the task she is suited to do, of course. Is this not so on your world?"

"Yes, I suppose it is." Prechard remembered vividly the night from out of her childhood — indeed, the last night of her childhood — when the men in green uniforms came to her house and told her parents that on the basis of her alfazeta test, they were taking her off to serve as a Planetary Explorer. "But in what manner is this determined on Khaton? What sort of test do you use?"

"Test?" Camas looked confused. "I don't know what you mean, Prechard. Each of us does what she does. It is that simple."

"Well," Prechard tried again, "how do you determine this?"

Camas shrugged. "By no means except that one is who she is."

"That doesn't answer my question," grumbled Prechard. "I can tell that it's going to take a lot of work for us to learn how to understand each other."

Camas brightened. "Indeed, Prechard," she touched her arm impulsively, "that is exactly what we must do."

Prechard and Camas laughed together, as they pressed the wet leatherleaf into pliancy.

3

Korith and Dennivan sat on the bank of a stream basking in the warmth of the afternoon suns with Ganvyla and her two children. The older child was wading in the slow running water and poking at mud grubs with a long stick. Ganvyla lay on her back drowsing, while Korith tossed about the baby who squealed and gurgled with delight. Suddenly, he turned to Ganvyla and asked abruptly, "Where's their father?"

Ganvyla opened one eye and looked at him. "Their what?"

"Their father? Where are the fathers of these kids?"

Ganvyla closed her eye and mumbled, "The Mother is the inspiration for life on Khaton. As the flower dreams its way to fruit, so The Mother brings the spirit to new life."

"I wasn't getting esoteric," said Korith. "I was talking about breeding."

They were interrupted, as a group of children, laughing and shrieking, raced toward them and plunged down the bank into the water. Ganvyla sat up and shook her head in annoyance, as water splashed cold against her sun-warmed skin. "Leave my body to the suns, seedlings," she admonished the children. Still laughing, the children moved downstream, and Ganvyla lay back again.

Pahma followed the group of youngsters, the rounds of her body jiggling as she trotted down the slight slope. Panting, she sat down beside Ganvyla and took her hand, pressing it against her cheek.

Ganvyla opened her eyes and raised herself up on her elbows. She smiled at the other woman. "Many slow hours have passed swiftly now," she said.

"Greetings again," Pahma returned her smile, then looked over at the men. "Greetings to you, Korith, and to you, Dennivan."

The men returned greetings, and Korith resumed his line of questioning. He pointed to the group of children splashing downstream and addressed Pahma, "Are any of those children yours?"

Pahma laughed, a deep, throaty sound. "No, Korith. My two oldest daughters serve with their aunt Amaranth and my youngest is helper to Amanita. And you, Korith, Dennivan, have you brought no offspring of your own?"

Korith and Dennivan looked at one another. "No, Pahma, we have no children," Korith answered.

"Indeed," acknowledged Pahma. Then she continued, "I have come to ask if the both of you would be pleased to take the evening meal with us in our chambers?"

Dennivan chuckled. "Some portions of our conversation may be confusing, but this is unmistakably a dinner invitation, and I accept, thank you."

"And I, too," Korith gave himself up the lure of friendship.

The air began to cool, and, as if on signal, Pahma scooped up the baby, and they all were suddenly standing, then moving up the hill. They walked briskly across a field, as the suns descended lower. At last they turned onto a path which led through a stand of trees and in among the series of chambers where the women lived.

The two little ones were whisked away by an older child, and the four adults continued to a large, open area. A stone fireplace stood next to a long wooden table on which were arranged sets of dishes, containers, and a variety of implements of different types. "Relax, sisters," Pahma motioned Korith and Dennivan toward comfortable looking seats. "Ganvyla and myself will prepare a fine guesting in your honor and to our new friendship." She moved behind a drapery and the two men sank down, sighing, relaxing in the warm, fragrant air of the chamber.

Ganvyla thrust a long stick among the grey chunks in the bottom of the fireplace. A spurt of blue flame flared high for a moment, then died down. The grey chunks began to glow, and Ganvyla removed the stick and set a round pan of oil over the coals. While the oil was beginning to sputter, she quickly mixed ingredients from various containers in a large wooden bowl which she then carried over to a cluster of tall, scarlet, trumpet-shaped flowers. She bent several half-opened blooms over her bowl, pouring in an amber liquid. All this she mixed rapidly, then dropped handfuls of it into the hot oil.

Pahma reappeared pulling a huge gourd on three wooden wheels. From a tap that was set into the gourd near the bottom, she drew four tall goblets of a frothy, deep orange fluid, and these she handed around. Korith and Dennivan sipped gingerly, then drank with relish. That the beverage was an intoxicant there was no doubt, yet the flavor was mellow with no trace of harshness or bite. It passed smoothly over the tongue and down the throat, soothing away any dryness and delighting the sense of taste with a rare freshness.

Ganvyla turned the frying cakes with a long stick and served them hot and crisp accompanied by cold spears of green shoots dressed with a piquant sauce. There were nuts and dried fruit from the last Harvest, and always more of the orange drink, until everything seemed to the eyes of the men to be haloed by a soft and fuzzy glow.

Several times during the course of the meal, strange women and girls would pass through the area. They would hesitate just long enough for introductions; the real sharing remained between Pahma and Ganvyla, Korith and Dennivan. The men spoke of their travels among the planets, and the women told about sometime journeys to the Great Forests riding the winds of fourth season in pods gathered during late Harvest.

Dennivan described his home planet — an arid world with vast deserts of brilliant colored sands and towering mountains which cupped protectively the few fertile valleys. He spoke of his restlessness, of the stirring in his blood which was the force behind his applying for service with the United Planetary Explorers.

Korith watched Dennivan, as he spoke, moving his hands about in accompaniment to his words. Korith stared at his friend's hands — Dennivan's hands, capable, graceful hands. Korith started with a thrill of recollected terror, and his own hand automatically stroked as if to sooth that which served him as a leg. Dennivan's hands, quick to cut away the rising corruption which fountained agonizingly from the place on his ankle where a tiny insect had suddenly stung him, had been gently firm, holding him, doing their best to comfort and to heal him.

Korith gulped at the orange drink. Cold sweat beaded on his forehead and upper lip. He raised his gaze to Dennivan's face and felt a warm relief at seeing the familiar fluff of hair framing strong contours of cheek, brow, and chin; the wide, smiling eyes set perfectly to each side of Dennivan's nose; his gentle mouth still moving with conversation. Korith smiled at the dearness of his friend—an unexpected feeling, intense and unfamiliar; a strangeness which grew quickly into fear and then was shattered by a thrust of denial that wrenched a gasp from Korith.

He looked around. Dennivan had stopped speaking and was examining a yellow crystal. Ganvyla had moved close to Pahma, and now she stood up. "It has been a most pleasant guesting, Korith, Dennivan." She pointed to a thick curtain of green vines bearing flowers of bright pink and scarlet. "Yonder chamber will serve for your retirement. Pahma, myself, we will depart to our own. Until the suns, then, again."

Korith felt Dennivan's eyes on him, and he was unable to meet them with his own. A tiny chill ran through him, and he struggled to his feet. "Guess I'll do some sleeping," he said, attempting a nonchalance that was far from what he felt. He did not look at Dennivan as he crossed the floor of the chamber, staggering slightly. He thrust himself past the flowering curtain and down onto the first pallet he saw. There, he rolled over onto his side and swiftly found the dreamless sleep he sought.

4

Captain Eliat lay on his back. He stared wide-eyed into the darkness of his chamber and allowed his body to enjoy the pleasant feeling of weariness laid to rest just short of fatigue. With an objective detachment, he began to review the events of the day. He sighed and shifted his position on the firm mat, as he thought about the tapple-withs and automatically suppressed a shudder.

It had been difficult for him to not show his disgust at the first sight of the great grublike creatures. Their shapeless, gross bodies were white and slimy, and a single ridge down the length of each sprouted long cilia which were used to penetrate the tender inner stems of the large fern in which they lived. They curled up five or six together in the center of the springing fronds, and their soft, moist bodies sheltered the developing flower in the heart of the plant, while through their cilia they absorbed nutrients that were being carried to the leaves.

As the tapple-withs grew ready to spin their cocoons, they exuded a thick latex which beaded on their skin. A skilled milker could skim off extra latex for her own use without disturbing the life cycle of the creature. "The tapple-withs change in their cocoons," explained Amaranth, "and they rise during the fourth season. They breed rapidly, and then each adult lays her egg in the empty seed case of the budaberry which protects them through the cold of fifth season. The eggs hatch early during the Season of the First Green, and the tapple-withs crawl out of the budaberry to seek communion with others like themselves."

Captain Eliat stared at her, as she spoke, watching the movements of her lips and tongue and noticing the perfection of her flashing teeth. Slowly he drew his eyes over the planes of her face, down the curve of her jaw, along the graceful line of her neck to the sweet hollow at her shoulder where the gold of her skin met the green border on her tunic. He wondered about the marriage customs of these people. Perhaps their men lived, unmentionable, in separate villages until the proper time for mating. He speculated about their men — where they were and what they were like — and he wondered in secret even from himself about Amaranth and mating, Amaranth and himself.

After the milker and her two young apprentices had finished their work, they bore away Amaranth and the two men to a huge chamber surrounded by spicy smelling bushes. Captain Eliat was introduced to women and to children, singing and dancing, food and drink, sounds and smells, until he felt as if his head might spin off his neck. He looked around for Lester only to remember that his crewman had made apologies and returned to his own chamber before they reached this one. The suns went down, and small fires with flames of different colors were kindled. Darkness closed over, and the lilac and amber moons began their sets of passes through the night sky over Khaton. Sometime, Captain Eliat remembered, Amaranth had bid him goodnight. Then two young children had him by the hands and were leading him through the darkness to his chamber.

Captain Eliat sighed, closed his eyes, and slept.

5

Robwill rolled over, smacked his lips, and opened his eyes. Pale early morning light filtered through the woven leaf and fabric which made up the roof of his chamber. He stretched, feeling the strength of his lithe body, still soft-skinned and rosy with youth. For an instant, he rejoiced in the freedom of his unclothed flesh. Then he rose, washed, and donned his uniform.

Robwill ducked beneath the door flap and into the clearing around which the chambers of the men were woven. A low fire was burning within the circle of stones, and over the fire hung a tall kettle. Near the fireplace, Lester sat on the ground sipping from a heavy mug. Robwill picked up a mug for himself from a heap of dishes near the fireplace and filled it from the kettle. The hot, green liquid was slightly bitter and very stimulating, and Robwill felt the last cobwebs of sleep melt from his mind. He glanced at Lester, wanting conversation but hesitating to disturb the older man's thoughts.

Lester took a long swallow from his cup, then spoke, still staring into the fire. "Been having some really strange dreams."

Robwill was silent. A response was not called for. Lester looked up at him and grimaced. "Wish I could remember what they were about. They sure were long and heavy through my sleep." He stood up, spilled the dregs of his drink on the ground, and rinsed his mug at the trough near the pile of dishes, then tossed it back on the heap. He began to leave the clearing, then stopped and looked back at Robwill. "Coming?"

Robwill thrilled at the invitation from his crewmate. He scrambled up, gulping the rest of his drink, and dropped his mug on the ground as he hurried to join Lester who was striding away.

Lester and Robwill followed the path past the chambers of Amaranth and on through the thick greenery. They stopped for a while beside a dark pool to watch tiny, rainbow-winged bugs skim about on the surface of the water, then continued along the path until they reached a point where it branched in five directions. Without hesitating, Lester turned onto the narrow track which ran off to the left, and Robwill followed. They kept to this course until they were brought up abruptly against the rocky face of a low cliff. There was a jagged opening in this wall, and Lester squeezed through, Robwill behind him. The older man did not speak, and the younger was reluctant to break the silence. They passed through a series of narrow tunnels and then out into an area which was open to the sky. Lester stopped, his breath rasping loudly, and Robwill stepped up beside him, staring.

The priest Amanita sat before a large brazier, while a young girl worked at a long bench set against a section of stone carved into a series of deep shelves and niches.

Amanita looked slowly up the length of Lester's body, then glanced cursorily at his companion. "So," she said, her eyes returning to grip Lester's, "here you are."

Lester held his gaze steady, nostrils flared with the effort. Robwill moved away from this tension toward the girl who smiled at him. She was crumbling dried leaves between her fingers. "What is that?" he indicated the herb.

"Thage, dried before it flowers." She packed the crushed leaves into a pouch. "It is for Dasay. I, Cyrall, go now to bring it to her. And you?"

"I, Robwill, happened here with my companion."

"Will you come with me to find Dasay?"

Robwill glanced over at Lester who was still gaze-locked with the priest. Something was happening that Robwill felt did not include him; yet here he was. "I would come, yes," he said to the girl—anything to get away from that tension he felt building, the strangeness that was so alienating.

6

"So, Lester?" Amanita's question was low, insisting, almost seductive. Her skin was the color and texture of ivory, her ruby eyes burned like fiery pits, but the pink down of her brows, lashes, and hair was all softness.

Lester waited, silent, refusing to give her the tiniest response. One corner of the priest's pale lips twitched slightly, and she stood and walked over to the workbench. "Will you have some guara?" She poured a cup of steaming green liquid and held it out, offering it to Lester.

Lester shook his head. A chill fluttered about his belly, and his voice caught as he tried to reply. He cleared his throat. "Thank you, but I have had mine already this morning." And I don't trust yours, remained unspoken.

Amanita shrugged, took the mug with her, and seated herself again by the brazier. She motioned with her head for Lester to sit down, as she sipped the hot drink.

Despite his desire to remain standing, Lester found himself squatting, then sitting on the ground across from the priest. He glanced at the burning coals, then tore his eyes away, as a cold anxiety began to build inside him. Amanita spoke, her eyes fixed on the low fire. "Are you whole, Lester?"

Lester twitched. "What does that mean?" He felt anger beginning.

The priest chuckled. "Being is more than merely life; and life is more than simply breath. If you will be whole, Lester, you must cease to fear becoming more than you are."

Lester's anger flared, and he leaned forward. "Do not seek to preach to me, woman," he said tightly. "Tell me, better, what of yourselves, and where are your men."

Amanita met his gaze. "Be you patient, Lester," she replied, "and I am certain that you will find that which you seek."

"I have dreamed strange," Lester held his voice steady. "Is this of your sending, priest?"

"Ask, instead, yourself, what comes at your own invitation." Amanita rose and deposited the now empty mug on the workbench. Then she reached into a niche in the rock wall and removed a small pinch of coarse orange powder. She returned to the brazier and dropped the powder in among the coals.

Lester recoiled as a tendril of thick smoke curled upward, spreading into a thin cloud which tantalized his nostrils with an exquisite perfume.

In spite of his anxiety, Lester leaned forward, and the smoke rushed up at him. He felt a drawing, a beckoning, and he followed. A heavy mist rose before him pierced by two glittering points of scarlet, and Lester stepped toward them. The lights grew into vast red pools which began to spin and whirl, yanking Lester suddenly into a vortex from which he shrieked to be free.

Just as suddenly, he was eased, soothed, gathered against a protective bosom, and he realized the presence of The Mother. /What do you fear from me, strange my child of the flesh?/

. . . . Lester whimpered. He was standing alone on a great plain. A blue sun shone down fiercely, and there were neither trees nor rocks to cast any shade. A harsh screech cut through the silence, and Lester threw back his head in time to see a gigantic bird descending at his face. Then the great talons struck and ripped downward, tearing Lester's face from his head and his genitals from his groin. The cruel beak ravaged his entrails, and his heart exploded in a blinding flash of light.

Lester opened his eyes. A small green lizard sat facing him. "Do not be afraid," it said. "Accept your fear. Invite it in, and it will graciously decline; for fear is a solitary creature which thrives on loneliness and doubts that cause it not to whither." Then it sprang at him and buried its fangs in his throat.

His eyes were filled with dark, and he smelled the must of underground. He reached out with his hands and touched stone imbedded in earth and continued his fingertip exploration to find only more of the same. He felt up the wall which arched over his head and continued down the other side to the floor. His hand dislodged a small rock which glanced off his shoulder, hurting him. More rocks began to fall along with a shower of dirt, and Lester felt about frantically. His fingers discovered nothingness near the floor, then grasped at the outlines of an opening—a passageway large enough to permit his prone body to enter. He squeezed his way in, as the chamber collapsed where he had been. Desperately he pulled his way forward, and rocks fell behind him as he moved, sealing the passage. A Way Out—he knew there had to be a Way Out. At the same time, he was certain that he would circle around behind himself only to come back upon the ruin which followed him.

Frantically, he continued to pull himself ahead of the falling rocks, until his tattered skin hung in shreds from knee to toe, from wrist to elbow; until the entire universe resolved itself into a torment of movement with no concept of anything other.

Lester floated on his back in a dense ocean of blue. Nearby a large pink whale lolled, smiling and spouting an occasional jet of spray. Lester laughed, as a gentle joy washed him inside and out, laving away all his hurts. He paddled over to the huge eye of the whale and looked inside. He saw himself!

He was seated in a large auditorium facing a podium upon which spoke a thin gentleman wearing a dark suit and top hat. "Let me once again reiterate," gurgled the speaker, "that the initial merging is always difficult to achieve because of the coded-in fear of obliteration." Applause swelled from the audience, and Lester leaned back.

The woman cradled his head gently in her lap and brushed his lips softly with her own. The rest of his body crackled over a cooking fire across the room, while a small, grimy person tended the spit and basted the meat. The woman kissed Lester's cheek, then whispered in his ear. She offered him a piece of meat on a skewer.

Lester turned around in his chair and belched. He set his drink down on the redi-table that floated to meet him and puffed contentedly on a grati-stick. Idly, he leafed through a

book on his desk. The doorbell rang. Lester saw his visitor.
"Come in," he said. . . . . . .

7

Robwill followed Cyrall up a winding path that led to the top of
a wide plateau. Here a group of women were working among tall
plants which were topped with thick, pink, fleshy flowers. Some of
the women were using long, thin tools to split the upper surface of
the flower petals, allowing a thick sap to ooze forth. The sap
rapidly dried into shining filaments which the women then drew
over the petals and leaves, where the fibers hung in great loops.

"The sap dries into cords and tightens, pulling up the seeds,"
explained Cyrall. "Once the seeds have fallen, we can take the sweet
fibers for our own use. Here comes Dasay now. Many greetings,
older sister," she addressed a woman who was approaching them.

"Many greetings," replied the woman. The color of her skin was
deep brown, her eyes were black, and orange hair flowed over her
shoulders and down her back. She smiled at Robwill, then at
Cyrall. "For the herbs, many thanks."

Cyrall handed Dasay the bag of thage, and the two women
clasped fingers together about the small object. "Are you preparing
for your journey, older sister?"

"I have begun to finish out my cycles. I would have this tea with
me when I go." Dasay swung the bag of herbs.

Robwill stared curiously at the woman. "Where are you going?"
he interjected.

Dasay stared back at him. "On your world, strange one, do not
the sisters go when it is their Time?"

"Time?" He felt compelled to make sense in his own mind of
what she was saying.

"When we of Khaton have reached our Time, we harness the largest pods for our transportation to the forests of the other continent. Each sister must go alone at her Time, there to meditate and seek the greater freedom."

Robwill looked uncertain, and Dasay continued, trying to explain, "These are my final seasons among my sisters. Before the season of cold arrives, I will seek my solitude. It is my Time."

At the mention of "final seasons," Robwill paled. These words recalled for him the court of Final Judgments on his home planet. This court, a prison labyrinth where the wealthy paid for a license to hunt, was where all common people were sent when their judgment was Penalty. "Do you suffer much then?" he blurted, completely personalizing her communication, not understanding her.

Dasay tucked the sack of herbs under her belt. "I attend to the beauty around me, strange sister. I have no time to suffer now for what has not yet come." She turned and strode back to the flowers.

"I must go to Amaranth's chambers now," said Cyrall to Robwill. "Would you come?"

Robwill shook his head, confusion beginning to dominate his thoughts. He was still hearing Dasay's words and turning them in his own mind into a struggle. He reached out for the security of familiar structure. "I'd better get back to the camp and see what the other guys are doing." His confusion focused into concern for the woman he had just met. "What did Dasay really mean about her Time? Is she going to die soon? Will she be hunted and tormented?"

Cyrall glanced at him, shrugged. "She will catch her pod from the Ban Yang and ride it to find her peace in the great forests. It is her Time." She moved down the path.

Robwill followed through the close brush, memories from his own past feeding his concern for the future of this strange woman. "Is it gruesome and depressing?" he asked Cyrall almost greedily. "Is she terrified?"

"Look, Robwill! The splendid creeper is in full flower!" Cyrall grasped his hand and pulled him toward a large tree which was wound round by pale, straw-colored vines bearing huge flowers of iridescent teal blue. Seven wide, thick, shimmering petals cupped each high mounded, furry, scarlet center; and from these soft hillocks, topping the petals, waved seven yellow tendrils scaled with deep orange. Cyrall reverently touched a blossom with a fingertip, then closed her eyes and drew the side of her face along the vine, caressing the flowers with her skin. The delicate, heady perfume of the plant rose to meet her eager nostrils, and she inhaled deeply, finding communion through fragrance. Then she stepped away, opened her eyes, and looked intensely at Robwill. "Fair afternoon, strange one. Do bring greetings from me to your other sisters." She inclined her body toward the splendid creeper and departed down the path towards Amaranth's chambers.

8

Robwill stood on the path, barely aware of Cyrall's departure. Dasay's voice still echoed between his ears, words winding through his own memories. 'Final seasons. My time. Final.' The sound grew louder, pressing out against his senses. 'It is My Time.' Dasay's voice became the voices of many women, sisters of Khaton. 'My Time . . . MY TIME . . . ' while the shining flower of the splendid creeper in Robwill's vision pulsated rhythmically to the chorus, growing with each word. Blue, yellow, and orange perfume filled Robwill's head and throat. He leaned toward the brilliant blossom, and seven orange-scaled, yellow tendrils beckoned to him and drew him in to its glowing heart:

/So you will know, dear strange my child./ Robwill felt the closeness of the Mother, and he had no fear, as his remaining worldly perceptions departed. /So you will know./

He became another:

Harnessed securely to the great pod, Hyassa rode the winds of fourth season. Pink strands of her hair streamed out behind like a company of banners against the sky, against clouds tinted lilac with changing amber shadows. Her mouth grinning into the wind squeezed her cheeks up, crushing them beneath her eyes.

The pod drove into a small spiral breeze, an updraft which spun them swiftly high, leaving Hyassa's breath momentarily beneath. Then she cried out, as the surge thrust her hard against the straps of the harness; spun cloud and sky, ground and leaf in a whirl before her vision, snatching her thoughts from her. She leaned her knees and inner thighs hard against the resilient flesh of the pod. The pod swelled to her pressure, singing its gorge of seed, glutted with new life to the point of bursting — and burst it would, spilling seed and perhaps Hyassa, too, into new life, new song.

But not yet. Hyassa stroked the pod's skin with her fingertips. *Not yet. First we must reach the forests; then we both may have our Time and the luxury of singing.* The pod dipped and soared, borne and bearing, erratic motion carrying always toward the forests and away from all pasts, away, and away.

Hyassa rested her chin on her chest, and sudden tears of her weeping briefly silvered the air. *It is My Time.* She threw her head back, facing into the rush of wind. Breezes blew through her open jaws scouring her tongue dry. Her lips curled high over her teeth, wide apart, spread to expose the pink scream of her throat. *Mine. My Time.* Air a gale in her mouth seared the private places inside her cheeks and the soft flesh at the base of her gums. She gagged, uvula glued against the back of her tongue, parched flesh sticking to itself. *I go toward. Forward.* Her lips floated together, quivered. Peeling skin reaching out for moisture stood high, brushed closing surfaces like butterfly feet. Saliva began to flow again, and Hyassa licked her mouth around the inside and then out and over her lips. She tilted her head to one side, and the warm gush of sorrow spilled down her cheek. *So why am I grieved? Why, then, do I weep?*

Hyassa slept and dreamed, her form draped over the body of the great pod. The pod continued forward, bobbing on, supported on air by the buoyant gas that was expelled by the seeds developing inside it.

The pod ascended, and Hyassa woke, light-headed from

thin air and fasting. They rode above clouds streaked with purple and orange. They flew ahead of the triple suns, but slowly; so that the great cluster of light gained on them until it passed them and continued ahead, moving over the horizon to leave the sky darkened for the paler show of the moons.

The air cooled, and the pod flew lower. Brush tips of shrubbery reflected light in pinpoints far below, as the moons chased each other by the pod, crossing the night with pastel shadows. Lilac and amber phosphorescence caught in sudden movement from a rippling surface of water. Moonlight played on it for a space of time, until the rising of the three suns illuminated miles of deep turquoise color which their combined light pulled from the sea.

Hyassa dozed and wakened until conscious thought no longer distracted her from being. She was, and she was, and the pod carried her on over the sea toward the greater continent.

Again stretches of land were beneath them — stark and rocky land with only occasional patches of vegetation. In the distance, beneath streaks of clouds colored pink, mauve, and pale orange, shone the jeweled colors of the forests. The suns rose high in the sky, shining on treetops in patches of red, purple, and green. Hyassa saw, and then she slept again.

She was jolted awake by a sharp cracking sound, and the pod lurched suddenly, throwing her against the straps. With a pop, a large fissure opened in the surface of the pod near Hyassa's thigh, and a series of black seeds, each perhaps the size of her fist, shot forth. Tiny filaments of golden silk blossomed from each seed, catching in the currents of the air and carrying the seeds away from the pod and from each other. The pod dropped sharply. There was another crack and pop, and another stream of seeds spurted, this time from the underside of the pod, followed by a third and fourth break.

The air became golden threadwork dotted with ebony through which shone the light from the suns broken into occasional rays of pure color by the brilliant web of seeds. Hyassa watched, enthralled, her face reflecting the glory of color. Then the entire pod exploded from beneath her, and she fell. Shreds of pod trailed from the harness that she still wore, and black seeds clung to the scraps and sprouted golden floss which snatched at the air to slow Hyassa's fall. Then the universe erupted into blinding no-color, sucked her in, and swallowed her.

Drift, float, ride the pulsations of the cosmos, wave of the ocean, formless, all-being, bliss.

Be wave of the ocean, formless, all-being, bliss.

Be.

Arrives fear and trepidation.

I.

Being is.

Am.

Doubt is; and trembling.

Casting out for solace, for comfort, and for clarity, one who is no longer the Source calls to the Source, reaching for knowledge from memory:

"Hylantree, Mother, lend me the staff of your wisdom to support me. Help me to find within myself the seed of the many-petaled flower which grows ever toward her reflection in the light and darkness of pure truth. Aid me, Mother, in my need, my confusion, my fear."

Faintly, the response:

/What troubles dear my child of flesh?/

"Mother, I am afraid. Ahead there is pain."

/The choice to go ahead or to remain is yours, dear my child, and only you may choose which end to pursue./

"And what choice is that, Mother?" angry. "If I stay or if I go, I still must go."

/This choice is yours—to remain or to go. It is your Time, and you must do or not do this thing alone. The next time you seek me as Hylantree, you must be Hylantree./

"Mother, I am not ready!"

Silence.

"Mother, I am afraid!"

Silence.

"Mother!"

Breathing hurt. Breathing was movement, and movement hurt. Hyassa moaned. She hurt. Light scored her eyes even through the closed lids. She felt a great heat on her face and rolled over to protect it with her arms. Rocks pushed against her belly, digging into her flesh. Sweat rolled down her body, stinging in cuts and scrapes where minute particles of the planet's surface had torn and become imbedded. Her nose and mouth were full of grit, and she coughed. Coughing hurt her.

She opened her eyes, then slitted them, as copious tears tried to wash out the intrusion of light. With an effort, Hyassa pushed herself up to sit. Her clothing had been stripped ragged in her fall, and beneath the tattered pieces of fabric, her flesh was patched with raw spots and bruises. Her parcels were gone — all her carefully packed teas, her warm robe, Ixoray's tool (the one keepsake she had allowed herself), and her own tools had been scattered in her fall and lost. She looked about, impressions swimming and blurring in her vision, then clearing.

She sat amid stones on a stark plain of grey sand crusted with red boulders. Here and there grew small clumps of a coarse-looking vegetation. In the distance shone the treetops of the great forest, while closer to her — Hyassa's heart leaped at the sight — was a stand of short trees which shaded mossy hillocks, a promising-looking oasis.

Hyassa's thoughts burst with recollections from her life past of soft forest mosses, cool and welcoming, of yielding ground like billowy cushions for the resting of her body. She yearned toward this now small place of promise for healing and soothing of her weary aches. The trees called to her of coolness and comfort, aroused memories of celebration with her sisters beneath the huge crown of flowers atop the Hylan-tree. The skin of her palm and fingers warmed to the recollection of Ixoray's hand holding her own, mounds and creases fitting together comfortably, like the bodies of two old lovers. Ixoray, sister of her, Hyassa's, heart, whose Time came early, before Hyassa's Time, smiled through pasts in Hyassa's thoughts.

Hyassa rose to her feet, her eyes fixed on the little cluster of trees. With a small cry, she raced over the dry ground, swift feet dusting clouds to rise trailing her across the plain. She dashed in among the trees and flung herself down at the base of a large trunk, burrowing against the heavy moss.

But the ground was hard and full of lumps. It bruised her sore flesh. The moss was not soft, either, but dry and scratchy. It abraded her torn skin; while great roots from the tree poked up through the dirt, exuding a sticky sap which burned her painfully where it came in contact with her flesh. "No," she wept, all fantasy shattered, "this is no friendly wood! There is no welcome here for me!" She shook with grief, and harsh cries were forced from her throat by the impact of loss.

Then she smelled water, and she needed it. The press at her senses pushed aside her feelings of desolation. She cast about urgently, her throat contracting, scratched surfaces rasping together.

She would have flung herself down to luxuriate in the water when she found it, had it been more than a tiny puddle, or, even then, had it not been covered with a pulpy grey scum. Hyassa pushed the ooze from the surface of the puddle, scraping it up onto the surrounding mash of land. She bent to the water with the strangeness of caution — the plentiful springs in the world of her days before this ran free and were always sweet to drink. This water stank, and even though the stench irritated her thirst, she could not bring herself to touch the water with her lips. She wiped her hand on a shred of the fabric which hung about her and backed away from the puddle, a sense of futility filling her, swallowing up even the fear and grief and pain.

Hyassa moaned, and the sound grew to a wail, long, loud, and horrible:

WAIL

Discord penetrates the universe, forcing apart molecules of substance until all existence rides on the vibration:

WAIL

Sound carries forth, shattering fear and darkness. Being rides in the folds of noise, rides out the end of the horn and into the cosmos:

WAIL

With the cry comes breath and a feeling of the flesh. Vibration recedes, gives way to other forms of experience:
Being.

Hyassa stood on the plain, her head thrown back, facing upwards. The air was working into a gentle breeze, bringing a coolness to Hyassa's skin. She watched a large bank of clouds hurtle from the horizon to overhead, spreading rapidly across the sky, darkening the day as it hid the suns. The darkness was sliced through by a bolt of orange lightening followed by a short cracking sound and a delicate perfume. Then more lightening veined the sky with purple, orange, and white, each color bringing an individual fragrance to the air.

Hyassa stood spellbound by the storm. Then sound and light faded, and the first drops of cool, pure water fell against her face. Hyassa stretched her arms out, welcoming the deluge. She stripped away the remaining tatters of clothing which still clung to her body and rubbed the welcome moisture against her skin, delighting in the feel of smoothness over her flesh. She ran her fingers through her hair, lifting the tresses to allow rain to wash through it, feeling sand and grit run down her back. She opened her eyes to the wet coolness and with her heart embraced the storm. . . . . . .

Robwill lay at the base of the forked tree which supported the splendid creeper. The sky was streaked with orange and violet from the rays of the setting suns, and the cooling air brought fragrant rain to shower upon Robwill. He turned his face up to the fall of drops against his skin and sighed deeply, as consciousness returned. He opened his eyes and looked upon the nearest flower to his field of vision. Radiant leaves pulled together, folded over scarlet centers, as the flowers closed for the night.

Robwill rose slowly, carefully, thinking that surely he must be stiff and sore from spending the afternoon curled up on the ground against a tree trunk, but his body felt good, and his thoughts were light. He did not remember the substance of his dream, but the sum of its feelings remained with him, even after he returned to the chambers of the men.

9

"A what?" asked Captain Eliat.

"Flacks jumping." Amaranth turned to the messenger. "Tell Celandine that I will be there soon. Perhaps the strangers will join us." She repeated the request to Danal and the captain: "Celandine has filled the flacks pits, and now she sends invitation to all who want to jump. We weave threads from the flacks, and to get them we have to stamp on the leaves and beat them to release the fiber. Would you like to come with us?"

"Sure," the captain said, although secretly he was annoyed at the interruption, even as he had been annoyed with Danal for asking to come along when the captain announced to the others that he was going to speak with Amaranth. He wanted to be alone with her, although his reasons for wanting this were beyond his considerations.

Danal frowned openly. He had come here with the captain on the chance of perhaps running into Vitis, but Amaranth was alone, and he found the subsequent conversation between her and Captain Eliat boring and stilted. "May as well," he agreed.

"Let's go, then." Amaranth led the men out of her chambers and through the forest. As they approached the flacks pits, the men saw women and girls jumping around in shallow ditches filled with long, fleshy-looking leaves. The leaves were springy, and the people bounced about, while they beat the surface beneath them with their feet and with wooden clubs held in their hands. Amaranth waved and laughed. She picked up a club from the ground and gave it to Danal, then found a club for the captain and one for herself. She ran to an unoccupied pit of leaves, beckoning for the men to join her.

Captain Eliat clucked with annoyance. Amaranth behaved in an unbecoming common manner when among her subjects. He tried to remind himself that different cultures have different customs, but one which always remained the same was that leaders everywhere acted in a manner that commanded respect — respect from both commoners and nobility. He decided that it must come from being a simple, tribal woman—most likely her mate or her father or the real leader for whom she stood in soon would return to take proper charge—and he forgave her. He watched her jump. She wore a short, sleeveless tunic of turquoise embroidered with gold flowers that caught and reflected the highlights of the skin of her bare arms and legs. The hem of her tunic whipped up and down as she jumped, revealing the soft flesh of her upper thighs as it swelled over her long muscles. Turquoise fabric pulled tightly over her shoulders, back, and breasts, in turn, as she swung her stick in rhythm with her jumping; and Captain Eliat could not tear his gaze from the easy movements of her body. Danal jumped across from her, and next to them a tiny, rosy child with great black eyes sprang about, laughing with glee.

Amaranth looked over at the captain. "Well, stranger," she called, "are you jumping?" Captain Eliat leaped into the pit and began to jump, beating vigorously at the leaves with his club. The work was harder and more demanding than it appeared, and the captain found it was necessary to concentrate on working out a rhythm of jump and swing. He soon was out of breath, but he would not permit himself to rest in front of Amaranth, and he hid his gasps for air.

Danal's face was flushed, and the captain was sweating heavily by the time the flacks broke apart under their combined blows into thick ropes of fibers. Amaranth cried out in triumph and flung her club in a high arc onto the bank. Then she sprang from the pit, motioning for the men to follow her. They climbed out more slowly and carried their clubs up the bank where they dropped them on the ground with the others.

Groups of women and girls were gathering around a huge pot, where Celandine, dark and wispy, was serving out a hot and savory-smelling stew. Danal was ravenous from the exercise. He took his bowl and sat alone, leaning against a tree, tired. He ate, intent on his meal for a while; then he chewed more slowly and watched the people around him. Captain Eliat had retired to a space beneath some trees with Amaranth and two other women, and he talked animatedly while the others ate. Danal's eyes followed the groups and clusters and individuals around to the stew pot, to Celandine who was speaking with—he gave a sudden start—

Vitis. As he stared, Vitis nodded, then turned and began to walk away from the diners, away from the flacks pits, away from Danal. Scarcely aware of the actions of his body, Danal set his bowl down on the ground, rose, and hastened past the groups of people to follow Vitis into the forest.

10

"Wait," called Danal.

Vitis turned, saw him, smiled. "Greetings, Danal."

Words fell out of his mouth. "I thought we might go for a walk or something," he said, not thinking at all.

She took him by the arm. "Come, then, to the orchard with me, since that is where I am going." She steered him past a series of chambers that ascended vertically into a huge tree, then across a stone arc bridge over a wide stream. They passed through a grove of spindly saplings, over a rise, and into a large field that was planted with trees in irregular rows and clusters. The evening was very fair, but throughout the length of the walk, Danal was aware only of the greater fairness of the woman beside him.

Vitis released his arm, closed her eyes, and breathed deeply. "Smell this perfume," she sighed. "All is in flower now. It is second season. Soon the flowers will give us their petals to make room for the swelling fruit."

Danal stared at the dark planes of her face, stared at the curve of her neck as she arched her head back, stared at the rise and fall of her full bosom. She opened her eyes, seeing him look, and he flushed with embarrassment.

Vitis seemed not to notice his blushing. She sat down on the soft grass of the hillside, and Danal sat next to her. Although the sun shone on them and the air was warm, Danal felt as though his skin were coated with cold grease, and trickles of icy sweat ran from under his arms and spurted from his palms. His heart began to thud unevenly, every beat seeming to dredge its energy from the depths of his bowels up through his belly, and his lungs constricted, causing him to pant for breath. He was aware of the nearness of Vitis with every exquisitely painful atom of his being, and he turned to her. He felt a current flow between them, drawing him helplessly closer, whimpering, until with a low cry, he pressed his lips to her mouth in one sudden move. Then he threw himself back and away, suddenly ashamed, and plucked nervously at the grass. "Forgive me, lady," he stammered, "I did not mean to take such a liberty."

Vitis laughed gently and touched the backs of her fingers against her lips. "Tell me, strange one, do not the sisters on your world pleasure one another with their bodies?"

Danal looked up, a strange hope beginning to swell within him. "Truly we do, but I am ignorant of the customs on your world. Tell me."

"You are strange, indeed, Danal. I can seek your soul with my own, but I do not find the blending that comes with commonalty. Rather do I find myself experiencing that which is familiar, yet different. We could not join as one to form still one but must, instead, bond as two to form yet another one. I must ponder this a while."

Danal shook his head, and his voice shook also, betraying his desire. "I do not understand of what you speak, fair Vitis, but if my words hold any meaning for you, let me say swiftly, before I lose my courage, that you are all beauty beyond words, and I love you."

"On Khaton," Vitis said, "it is usual for us to freely find joy and pleasure in whatever way we will with each other. And, for some of us, there is one special sister who is heart of our heart, soul of our soul. We may love many, but there remains this dearest sister to love beyond those who take our fancy."

Danal began to tremble. "And do I take your fancy?"

Vitis nodded. "Indeed, I find you attractive, and even, perhaps, in time, I may find you dear. Still, the threads of my heart's spirit are weft among the soul's strands of my most dearly beloved special sister."

"I don't understand," said Danal, who was suddenly, and to his great dismay, beginning to. "Do you mean that one of those other women is your lover?"

"Of course. How could it be otherwise?"

Despair smoked in Danal's gut and burst into a flaming anger. He grabbed Vitis by the arm, hurting her, and thrust his face close to hers. "And where are your men?" he demanded. "What of them? What of us?"

Vitis frowned, pushing his hand away. "Do not grab and crush me. Your words make no sense, and neither do your actions. My sister, what is your problem?"

"I am not your 'sister'!" Danal exploded. "I will show you action with sense! I am a man, do you hear? A man!" In a fury of frustration, he flung himself on Vitis, feeling an uncontrollable heat rise within him as he crushed her lips with his teeth. Frenzied, he tore her clothing, pinning her down with his own body so that she could only struggle beneath him; until, spent, he collapsed on top of her, then rolled to one side.

Throughout she made no sound. Now she touched her bruised mouth and pulled her shredded tunic together. "So," she said, wincing with the movement of her lips, "you are 'a man', and this, then, is your way. May the Great Mother have pity on you."

Danal sat up and clutched at her hand. "Please," he whispered, "forgive me, lady. I didn't mean to. Have I hurt you?"

"Yes," answered Vitis, meeting his eyes with such cold fury in her own that Danal cringed away from her. "You have hurt me. You have violated my body, and you have broken my trust. Go away, you." She clasped her arms around her knees and stared out over the flowering orchard, rocking herself gently and making little sounds of healing deep in her throat.

Shaking, Danal rose to his feet. "I'm sorry," he said again, more loudly. He felt a different kind of fear begin deep inside himself now.

"Yes," agreed Vitis. She looked at him again, her eyes orbs of shining violet power which Danal felt as though he were being tumbled towards. He closed his own eyes and quaked with vertigo, while his heart fluttered in terror. "Go away now, you."

Danal opened his eyes. He opened his mouth and tried to speak but gagged on the thickness of his tongue. Then he turned and scrambled away from the orchard and the woman who sat with her back to his departure.

11

Camas turned her head, as the light from the rising suns pried at her eyelids, waking her. She opened her eyes and pressed back against the spongy moss which cushioned her, stretching her body and reflecting on the oddness of her new friend. Prechard lay nearby, strange even in sleep. *She is of another world*, Camas turned the thought over in her mind as she scrubbed her scalp briskly, long ebony fingers dancing through the white fluff that covered her head. *Of another world*, her silver eyes tracked the angular length of the sleeper, *and so how different but, yet, how like she is*. Camas touched the corner of a smile with her fingers. *She came with me, and now here she is*.

Prechard muttered. Her hand twitched. Her eyelids twitched, and suddenly she came fully awake and bolted upright. Eyes wide, she stared around the hillside where she had slept. Then she saw Camas, and she remembered; and she burst into tears.

"Dear sister," Camas was suddenly concerned, "why do you weep?"

Prechard wiped her face, tears ceasing as quickly as they had begun. She looked intensely at her friend. "I weep with release. I weep from the losing of a pain that was so old I had forgotten that it was a pain at all, it had become such a part of me. When I saw your face in the firelight during the evening meal, I recalled the exhilaration of working with you through the day. Then a pang went through me which twisted my brain and racked my entrails, so that I remembered times long ago when I was little more than a child, when I had been snatched from my home to face my future, and a woman was soft with me, kind to me, and loving. Then, when you crossed the clearing and sat with me, I knew that all the time between then and now, all my life of preparation and of activity, was meaningless."

"Tell me, then," said Camas. "Tell me." She held Prechard, rocked her, comforted her, and she listened.

Prechard told Camas of her growing up, of her family, of warm feelings she remembered from her childhood. Then she reached an age to be Tested, to determine her future training; and although the explorers were of high prestige, she prayed that she would fail to score for this, because she did not want to leave her home. But she did score, and the men came to get her, and they took her to be trained for exploration of the planets. "I did not want to go," Prechard's voice was almost a whisper, and Camas could feel part of her old pain. "I did not want to leave my home. I did not want to travel and explore. I did not care for the prestige. I did not fit my Test, and so they all told me shame."

"Shame?" Camas stared at her, confronting her, holding her gaze with reflections in silver. "Who were they to tell you shame?"

"They didn't know. They didn't care. They took me when I wished to remain. They pressed me to their service, and when I struggled with my frustration and wept with the futility of my anger, they told me shame again. They matched me with a mate of their choosing to whom I must return when this mission is finished, with whom I must bear many children to please the State. They matched me with a mate whom I do not love, for whom I do not care, but to whom I must return — we have been assigned together."

Camas was incredulous. "And what if you won't?"

"We must do as they would have us do. If shame will not force us, then there is incarceration, and, at the last, mind-bending."

"And now, what if once again you would wish to remain?"

Prechard was very quiet for a moment. Then she looked around her and sighed. She laid her palm against the cheek of Camas and felt a feeling descend through her that was the beginning of a sense of peace. "Perhaps this time, sister of my heart, it will be different."

12

Softly, gently, Amaranth touched the bruises on the body of her friend. "Dearest one," she whispered, "how came these? Did you cruelly fall?"

Vitis winced slightly beneath Amaranth's light fingers. "No, I did not fall."

"How then?"

Vitis was silent for a long moment. Then she sighed. "Danal hurt me."

"How so?" Amaranth's voice was sharp.

"Dearest woman, my beloved, this poorest of sisters has a pressing evil within her which rises beyond her control."

Amaranth was very still. At last she spoke, her voice trembling, "Would that I could ease the sufferings of the stranger. Would that I could be a lamp against that pathetic darkness." Then her voice broke, and she breathed harshly, sobbing. "However," her voice became firm, hard, "Danal has harmed my dearest you, and now I shall indeed punish her!"

"No need for that, dearest Amaranth." Vitis touched her fingertips to Amaranth's lips, stroked her cheek, then slid her palm down to rest against a golden shoulder. She smiled ominously, with satisfaction. "Danal will indeed be punished," she said softly, "and at no cost to either of us. We need take upon ourselves no responsibility. I have simply turned her twisted sickness back on herself, and she will wallow in it alone, bringing punishment to herself. There is no need for any further consideration from either of us for Danal."

13

"Forgive me, lady," said Captain Eliat, "if I should break with any custom by speaking of your men, but one thing I must know, and that is if your mate and father of your children has any hold over you, if in fact he lives."

Amaranth regarded him cooly, copper eyes gazing at his face over the rim of her goblet as she drank. She took her time, trying to control her annoyance. She would have eaten her morning meal alone with Vitis but for the fact that this person had appeared in her arbors asking to see her: then, when she appeared, persisted in speaking riddles to her. At last she set down her goblet. "Explain to me once again what it is that you wish," she said carefully.

The captain breathed slowly, evenly, willing his thudding heart to quiet. How could he even begin to explain the compulsion that sent him to see her as soon as he had awakened—just to look upon her, to hear her voice? He wanted all and only her in the entire universe, over and above all else. In truth he had thought of nothing but her since first he opened his eyes that morning, and indeed she should feel the same about him; for wasn't he a Captain? "A beloved," he rasped, "have you, then, a beloved? Is this a word that holds meaning in reality for you? Do you have a beloved?"

Amaranth looked at him sharply. She understood his words, but she was not sure of his motives in asking. "Yes," she replied, "I do know of what you speak. I do have a beloved."

Captain Eliat felt a surge of hopelessness in his gut. "Well, then," he said, needing to use more words to cover the fact or, perhaps, to make it more real to himself, "who is he? Where is he? Why do you keep him hidden?"

"Nothing is hidden," answered Amaranth, "and all know the fact—the heart of my own heart's song is echoed by the heart of Vitis who is my very dearest."

Captain Eliat reflected on her words for a long moment. Then he frowned. "I should have foreseen this, I suppose, and I suppose it was to have been expected. I have heard of women who love one another, but that, assuredly, is because they lack enough men to go around. So where, then, are your men here?"

Amaranth shook her head. "Your words are strange. Are you truly so concerned with matters of form and body shapes? What matters it, if the spirit is that of the beloved?"

"You are a leader of Khaton," said the Captain, annoyed, "but you are still, as well, a woman; and woman has a need for that which only man can give her."

Amaranth glared at him, copper fire flaring. "Who are you," her voice was low and controlled, "what are you to even think to dare presume that you could give me more than I?"

Captain Eliat shrugged. "I am a man, and woman is bound to man by forces beyond her control." *As I would have you bound to me*, whispered his silent wish.

Amaranth's lips tightened over her teeth. "In this, dear sister," she said icily, "you are very much mistaken. You are you, and I am I; and whatever else we are, we are still these and these most of all."

"And I am a man; you are a woman," he said firmly, "and *this* is fact, and that is all."

Amaranth tossed her head back and laughed loudly. "I have need to tell you that you had best curtail your speech to others on Khaton, lest all on Khaton hear and know that you in truth can be both pompous and inane."

"And you," retorted the Captain, "reason with the fullness of feminine irrationality."

Amaranth frowned. "I am a sister of Khaton, and you are a guest, no matter that you are insulting to me. Therefore, I must temper my own speech and afford you the respect due to those who differ in custom. I will have no more harsh words with you, Captain Eliat."

The captain frowned. "As guest, then, I will demand that you listen to me as woman to man." He grabbed her by the arm.

Amaranth pulled herself free from his grip. "Do not seek to bind me," she said sharply, "and do not put your hands upon me in attempted restraint. On Khaton the custom is that we each be free from demands and conditions put to one from another. We do not attempt to impose our strength one over the other, and I will not permit this to be done by you, no matter how different your own customs." Her copper eyes shone with anger, and Captain Eliat felt her fury as an almost tangible pressure.

He retreated before her wrath. "I ask your pardon," he said stiffly. "I impose no conditions. I merely seek to explain myself."

"And I have tired, for now, of listening. Maybe another time, Captain Eliat." Carrying her goblet, Amaranth turned and strode from the arbors.

Cursing himself for losing his temper, cursing Amaranth for provoking him with her beauty, cursing Vitis who was her lover, and cursing this whole dizzy world full of women, Captain Eliat stormed off in the opposite direction.

14

Danal wandered among the flowering plants of Khaton, his senses registering the beauty of which his self was unaware. Shame burned within him, consuming, as his feet carried him through woodlands, over hills, and across fields and streams. The triple suns set and rose and again sank low in the sky, and Danal wandered away and about, quietly seeking what must be done.

What must be done? She will tell, and they will know, he thought, *and what will they do to me then*? Anxiety squirted from his stomach through his entire body, and a great weakness descended into his legs causing them to tremble and then to buckle, and he sank to the ground. *What will they do to me then*? The suns descended over the horizon, and a sudden chill struck through the grey twilight. Danal leaned against the ground, supporting himself, as the trembling spread into his arms and hands. His teeth began to chatter, and he wrapped his arms tightly about his knees and rocked back and forth, moaning. *And what will they do to me now*? The words circled through Danal's dimming awareness, as the lilac and amber moons rose high in the sky over Khaton. . . .

Danal broke from the tall grass and sprinted over the rough

ground toward the rocky face of the cliffs. His frantically searching eyes spotted a narrow ledge a third of the way up — surely it was not quite beyond his reach — which might offer him some protection, and perhaps from there he could make his way to the top of the cliff. A long howl sounded behind him, and he lowered his head, struggling to maintain his ultimate speed. Sweat stung his eyes. A thrill of panic jolted through him, as he stumbled, then regained his stride. His breath rasped raggedly from his chest and throat, as he fought to both continue his forward progress and yet manage to suppress the fear which swelled through him.

Now! He leaped, caught at the miniscule projections with his fingernails, clawed his way up to the ledge which was barely wide enough for him to sit on with his knees drawn up against his chest. Blood ran from his lacerated hands and knees, and the trembling of his body threatened to tumble him from his precarious perch.

Another howl broke the stillness, closer this time, followed by a high-pitched whine. Danal pressed his shoulders back hard against the stone, whimpering, buffeted by a whirling dizziness of terror that was all but absolute, as horror bounded from the grass toward him.

They were small — each rough, hairy, brownish-yellow body about the size of Danal's head, while their ten jointed legs were each perhaps as long as his arm. The oval bodies bobbled grotesquely up and down between these bristly appendages, as the creatures scurried over the rocky terrain toward the cliff. At the foremost point of the ovals, the cracked, scaly skin ended in a mound that was a bright, shiny, pink; moist and rubbery- looking. At the very center of this mound was a needle-toothed orifice ringed round by squirming, wet, red villi.

The creatures grunted and hissed, as they reached the cliff and jumped about beneath the ledge where Danal crouched, trying to scramble up to get him; and his guts constricted, squeezing his terror through his limbs, until it seeped from his skin as a thick mist which settled slowly over the creatures. Greedily they turned their eager openings toward the mist and sucked it in, and as the fog of Danal's fear grew thicker, the creatures below him grew larger and stronger and jumped higher.

"No!" Danal screamed his denial aloud. How dare they feed on his fear and grow strong! Anger exploded inside him, bursting from his pores as flashes of white light which penetrated the mist, striking the creatures as they fed. How dare they! Danal flung the barbs of fury at them, and they began to retreat.

Danal felt the beginnings of a gloating satisfaction which he allowed to mingle with his anger. He aimed his spears of energy carefully to hurt these creatures who had presumed to attack him. His eyes narrowed into slits, and he nourished the hate which throbbed and swelled in him, then short forth a blinding crimson shaft that with a single blow struck down all of the creatures below the ledge. Danal leaned forward, panting, and smiled tightly at the ruined bodies. The rod of his hate hovered over them, then twisted into a thick tendril which flew back at Danal and wrapped itself about his throat. With a strangled cry, Danal fell, and as he fell, he began to come apart. All pasts and futures ripped from him and away, and he fell and fell, his head ringing with the echoes of his own silent shrieks. He fell, and the last tatters of himself were torn away to flutter in ragged strips which separated, disintegrated, and then were not. . . . . . .

PART THREE

1

"It's been days!" sputtered Captain Eliat waving his arms about. "I mean, where is everybody?" He glared at Robwill.

Robwill looked away, a sudden fear for his Captain piercing the serenity which had eased his days since his dream. "Beg your pardon, sir," he ventured, "but I've been coming back here every night, and you are the first person I've seen. However, I have not been here by day, and the others might have returned then." He smiled in gentle recollection of days spent amid the beauty of Khaton, until sundown, when he again would return to his sense of being Space Explorer, and would go to the chambers of the men for his evening rituals and sleep. To his knowledge, he had been alone until this morning, when he went out from his chamber into the clearing to find his Captain.

Captain Eliat's thoughts whirled through the blur of past events. He remembered little save that his anger had grown after he left the chambers of Amaranth, obscuring his senses so that they brought him little reliable information from the experiences which followed. He could remember many women — that was all; that and the fact that he had seen no men nor any signs of man. "Well," he barked, and Robwill jumped, "I just need to do some thinking, get my thoughts in order. Gain a new perspective. That's it. I need to sort it all out. These women are insidious, Robwill. They will rob a man of his reason. I expect that the others will be returning shortly, eh, Robwill?"

"Yes, sir." Robwill chewed at the base of his thumb and watched the Captain pace back and forth in the clearing amid their chambers.

"I don't even know how long it's been!" Captain Eliat spun around to face Robwill. The younger man recoiled, as the Captain took a step toward him. "Do you realize that? I have lost count of the days, and I have radioed and called and have not found a band of communication for any of the others. I don't even know where they are!"

"Perhaps, sir, they'll show up shortly." Robwill had never seen Captain Eliat so anxious, and he tried to ease his own growing fear. The very structure of his existence was dependent on the strength of his Captain, and the fact that his Captain took responsibility for him.

Sensing Robwill's fear, Captain Eliat recovered his composure. It was most inappropriate for a Captain to lose control, especially when his men were depending on him. With an effort, he smoothed the lines from his brow and pulled himself up straight. "Perhaps they will," he said stiffly, then added almost as an afterthought, "Robwill."

Robwill smiled, feeling secure again at the sound of his name. "Yes, sir," he said. He resolved to spend the entire day with his Captain. "Will you have some guara, sir?"

2

Danal crouched naked outside the great door of the castle, head tilted back, watching dull spires scratch at the bleached skybowl above. *Strange, the clouds no longer swim about. Has time indeed been stilled at last?*

A low cry from the belly of the castle begins a rending of the heavy stillness, tears apart the fabric of the air and shatters the faded skybowl. From jagged gaps in the above, a murmur of many forlorn voices press through moist silence, whirl about Danal and pluck at the little hairs upon his skin, urging his melody to come forth and blend with their own. Slowly he rises and moves his feet one in search of the other. Each step repeating, he passes beneath the cold stone lintel, as the castle triumphs and swallows him.

Fear rolls in cold drops upon his skin, pours down the castle wall, oozes over the grey stone. Fear drips down the back of his throat, bitter, rising from his belly to obstruct his breath. Softly, tentatively, Danal feels about for what is the best of all possible beginnings. The voices from the prisons call to him, cry from the lofty towers and stone dungeon cells.

Danal throws his head back and breathes deeply, drawing the air of life within the castle into himself. His ears stare at the spread of many passages beyond the great hall, and he chooses a direction and moves into the first of the lesser corridors.

Danal moves, and fear flickers among crevices, seeps from the stone. From the center of the corridor a mighty cloud issues to block Danal's path. Thrusting itself about him, the cloud presses Danal to the ground, and he falls. He falls.

Danal rises from the sand. Nearby, a small, green lizard crouches, licking blood from its fangs and claws. Danal shivers and averts his gaze, follows the shoreline with steps, his feet splashing through the warm and shallow water. In the distance he sees the spouting spray from a whale, while the cries of sea birds sound in the clear air.

Suddenly his sense of smell rises to the aroma of roasting meat. His stomach contracts, and he casts about for the direction. His stomach leads him, and he searches to locate the gaping hole in the sand. From this fissure issues a profusion of tantalizing fragrances. Danal closes his eyes. He thrusts himself headfirst into the hole. He falls. Softly, he floats, directionless, extending self in delicate antennae which catch among the currents of the ether. Cautiously, he stretches forth silken tendrils of being which carry him on the winds of time toward awakening.

3

Amanita and Lester sat across from one another, a low, blue fire between them. As they sipped from mugs of hot guara, the lilac and amber moons moved across the black sky, causing changing patterns of gently tinted light and shadow to play among the rocks and over the ground.

Amanita cast her scarlet gaze at the man. "Be you ready, Lester," her voice was low. "Since you are prepared, when the moons are each at opposite horizons, you may receive the Oracle; and then you will know, Lester. All your questions will be answered, and you will know."

Lester was silent and drank his guara and waited. His thoughts were as empty as his belly, and he waited. He was barely aware of Amanita as a white smear against the night, moon hues changing about her as she rose and stepped into the soft light, moving about, doing. Lester waited and was, and the lilac and amber moons moved past one another in their pattern of revolution.

Amanita returned to the fire. She squatted next to Lester and opened her hand. He looked. On the flat of her palm lay three smooth, green pebbles. Slowly, Amanita closed her fingers over the pebbles and turned her hold over the blue embers, then dropped the three stones. A stream of green smoke issued from the heating pebbles, rose, expanded, and spread through the air. Lester closed his eyes.

/Wisdom upon wisdom, Truth upon truth: pyramids rotate to point, crash, topple, coalesce, manifest, liquify, evaporate, seep through the molecular universe and pry apart the different cells of similarities; rearranging, interchanging, until transcendence eliminates with a rush all divisions and all transitions. There can no longer be communication. There is only Knowledge. It is that Total:/

* * *

"Did everyone get through alright? No one is missing?" Lystrie's voice was sharp with anxiety. She looked swiftly about,counting, then smiled tightly, satisfied that they all had made it. "There." She set the activator and shut the door of the chamber, sending it onward so that they would not be traced. 'Nor can we return,' she thought, then spoke aloud again: "In haste we have chosen our future. May this world be for the better."

"A benediction," muttered Irin. He held tightly to the hands of Maddon and small K'ronna. "In truth, Lystrie, this was well done. *We* have escaped Kandor. Now we are here, and it can only be for the better."

J'mayya moved closer to Vango. "Somehow," she whispered, "you don't know what to expect in the end when you . . . flee." Her voice broke on the last word, and she swallowed a sob, as she looked desperately about at her companions.

Maddon, Irin and K'ronna stood huddled together, two pitifully small packages at their feet. Lystrie and Suth both wore backpacks and tool belts, while she and Vango each had managed to rescue their emergency packs. Dowe carried only baby S'dokay. Bileya was laden with equipment grabbed in haste, and the boy Malee held a parcel of foods.

"Vikado and Naranji were Caught," said Maddon in a tiny, choked voice, "and Kohay and all her family. And the others . . ." a sob burst from her throat, and she clapped a hand over her mouth.

"We have escaped Kandor!" Lystrie's voice was hard and flat, sounding loudly in the strange air. "All that was is behind us, never to follow. Never! Look about you, my companions, and see the beauty of our new home!"

The others followed her gaze to the horizon where triple suns descending lit the sky with pink and orange fire. The people watched in unabashed wonder, open-mouthed, breathless, as slowly, slowly, that great blaze moved to the edge where it seemed to hesitate for a fraction of a moment, then tipped majestically over the rim and sank from view, leaving glowing coals of clouds to softly light this new world for her newest population. A small lilac moon rising in the North tinted the evening shadows with violet.

The people began to murmur their thoughts, subdued, but with excitement beginning. Irin unwrapped a portoblaze, and although the evening air was warm and pleasant, they were grateful for the familiarity of the glaze-glo in this strange place. Suth had managed to bring a bubble, and the people set it up and crowded inside. Through the transparent dome of the shelter they watched the lilac moon nearing the far horizon while a larger amber-colored moon appeared in the Northern sky.

That first night the people mourned those friends lost to Kandor.

In the morning they explored for a short distance around the great clearing where they had set up the bubble. They found clean, running water and many varieties of lush and succulent plants bearing the last vestiges of flowers and the first traces of fruit. Later, they assembled for Service close to a gigantic tree which grew at the edge of the clearing. Bileya raised high the ogstone chalice filled with the water of this world. Then she lowered the cup to allow Vango to drop into the liquid a pinch of dark soil from the planet. She sipped from the chalice, then intoned the words of the blessing: "Thanks be to Khaton for helping us to deliver ourselves from the hands of our oppressor Kandor. We dedicate ourselves to a new life in the spirit of Khaton; thus we call this new world by the name of Khaton in praise of The One Who Is All That Is Not Kandor."

The others raised their voices in the ritual chorus, as they passed the chalice to allow everyone to drink. "All blessings! All blessings!"

* * *

Khaton treated the people kindly, sharing with them, meeting their needs, and they grew comfortable with this new world. They ate of the plentiful fruits, and, as the weather began to turn colder, dried these along with herbs. They stored roots and seeds, knowing nothing of how the time of cold on this planet would be. They built sturdy shelters of stone, earth, and wood, one for each family unit, at the base of a hill from which flowed a series of springs; and they collapsed the bubble and folded it back into its casing.

There came a period of dry and chilly weather, and then the rains began, heralding the season of first green. Suddenly the days were hot, steamy, and a vibrant verdancy shimmered over everything. Plants sent up their sap, and the first tentative leaflets appeared. Lystrie was delivered of a male child. The people ate of the plentiful new shoots and greens and were comfortable with Khaton.

There was a time when the world was filled with flowers, and then, swiftly it seemed, flowers dropped to reveal tiny fruits which grew and ripened and burst with the fullness of their seed. The climate was kind, and the people built new dwellings close to and among their sisters of the flower.

The ogstone chalice rested on a small stone altar before the Hylantree. Today the goblet contained the rich, dark juice pressed from the fruit of this great tree, and heaped on the stone about the chalice were fruits of many varieties and in all stages of ripeness. The Hylantree herself was heavy with fruit. She bore her crop of sweet globes throughout the season; they were the first to ripen and the last to go to seed.

Bileya stood beside the altar. "All blessings flow between us, Khaton," she intoned.

"All blessings," the people murmured together.

Bileya continued, "With joy and in celebration we realize the completion of one cycle of seasons. May the next cycle be as kind to us as this first one has been."

"All blessings, Khaton," the voices of the people rose in volume. Someone produced a hand twanger and began to plunk out a rhythm, while someone else blew on a set of pipes made from river reeds. Laughing, the people pranced and pirouetted about the Hylantree, and the mammoth plant seemed to dip and sway the tips of its branches in time with the dance. Malee began to sing:

Swell, fruit.
Shout joyfully your gorge of seed.
Burst with delight in your ripeness.
Scatter your hoard of new life for the sprouting.
Swell, fruit.
My throat aches with pleasure at the thought of your juice.

* * *

The orbit of the planet called Khaton was erratic, forming a series of irregular ellipses about the triple suns. As a result, the length of the seasons varied from one year to the next, depending on the path of each revolution. Thus it was that the second year the people lived there, the warmer seasons were longer than they were the year before, and the colder seasons were very short. During this time, J'mayya had a boy child, and Lystrie and Maddon became pregnant.

The warm seasons which followed this second winter were much shorter than the previous ones had been—nearly as short as the cold seasons which they followed. There was little rain, but even so, the plants produced a bounteous harvest. The people were frustrated by their inability to predict the length of the seasons, and they worked hard during a brief time of harvest, for they feared that the remainder of the year would be cold, and the winter especially bitter.

The weather grew colder, and there was frost, then heavy ice, then a great blizzard—the first snow the people had seen there. Their new homes were cold, and they again erected the almost forgotten bubble, crowding together inside in an attempt to keep warm at night. One bitterly chill morning, the air was filled with black dust—spores from the black fungus. That evening, the men began to die.

"J'mayya," called Vango, "come quickly and have a look at the boy!"

J'mayya put down the heavy strands of korfiber which she was twisting into a rope. "Here," she called. She blew on her chill-numbed hands and stooped slightly to enter the house through the low, stone-framed doorway. The greatroom was warm, heated by the fire which Vango had built up in preparation for dinner. She passed through the greatroom and into the smaller room which she and Vango shared with their child. Vango was holding the baby in his arms.

J'mayya felt a sudden fear bite through her, as she pushed close to them. "Here, let me see." The child lay still. His swollen eyes were closed, and his skin was greenish-grey. His breathing was rapid and shallow. "What?" J'mayya's cry was sharp.

Vango looked at her helplessly. "I bent over his bed to look upon him as he slept, and . . . and . . . I saw this." He closed his eyes and swayed. His breath caught, and he grabbed at the wall, then sank down on a low stool, still holding his son.

J'mayya's heart fluttered with panic, and she shook her head insistently from side to side in denial. "What is happening, Vango, with our son? And with you?"

Vango leaned his head against the wall. "Look to the baby, J'mayya. My own sudden weakness will pass."

J'mayya took the boy from Vango's arms. The tiny body felt stiff and somehow insubstantial, and as J'mayya held him, feeling deeply her own helplessness, the child's breathing began to labor, then suddenly stopped. J'mayya's head began to whirl, and she felt as though the entire room were revolving about her. Without conscious thought, she pressed her mouth against that of her son and attempted to force air into the tiny lungs. She was unaware of a knocking at the door—she knew only of the small, limp body which she somehow had to revive.

"J'mayya!" Bileya burst into the room. "Please, quickly! Malee and Dowe . . . " she stopped short.

J'mayya lifted her face from that of her son and looked blindly at the other woman. Bileya had been weeping, and her face was blotchy and swollen. "What?" J'mayya's question was dull, automatic.

Bileya shook her head, staring at the child J'mayya held. She opened her mouth, and a choking noise came forth. She crammed the knuckles of both hands against her teeth and burst into fresh tears. "What? What? What?" Her voice grew shrill and then broke off, and she began to tremble.

J'mayya stepped close to the other woman. She held the body of her baby cradled in one arm, grabbed Bileya's hair with her other hand, and shook her. "Tell me," her voice was a monotone. "Tell me."

Bileya stared wildly about the room. "I don't know," she said. "I just don't know. Malee came to me and leaned against my knee. I put my arm around him to hug him, and he slid to the floor. I bent over him, and he was dead. Just like that, J'mayya, he was dead." She spoke simply, like a small child. "I screamed for Dowe, and he didn't come. I picked up Malee and put him on the bed, and I screamed for Dowe, and when he didn't come yet, I went to look for him. He was outside, J'mayya. Dowe was outside in the snow, and he didn't come, because he was lying in the snow, and he was dead, too. He didn't answer me, J'mayya. He couldn't come, because he was dead, too."

"Vango?" J'mayya turned to the man. He remained seated on the stool leaning against the wall. His eyes were closed, and his face was colorless. "Vango?" J'mayya felt panic swelling through her. She walked over to him, each step repeating as though through an eternity. Vango's eyes remained closed. J'mayya, clutching the body of their child, reached out a trembling hand and touched Vango on the shoulder. His flesh was cold; his still body empty of life.

There was a terrible time then; a time of great sorrow and confusion. Suddenly, within a space of only minutes, the men all were dead, and the boy children also. There remained only J'mayya, Lystrie, Bileya and S'dokay, and Maddon and K'ronna. Lystrie and Maddon were both heavy in their pregnancies.

The women moved the corpses of the men and boys inside the walls of a commonhouse that had not been completed. There, they sang the Kaddish of Kandor, too numb with shock and fear to weep yet. After, they set a torch to the wood, and as the flames sprang to engulf the dead flesh, the women shed their first tears. Mourning, they went together to the house of J'mayya, and there they sought to make their peace with their tribulation.

Lystrie huddled around her swollen belly, stroking the huge mound almost desperately with both hands. She looked at the other women. Her eyes were ringed with dark circles which stood out sharply in her pale face. At last, she gave a small sigh and spoke. "I have not felt my child move in my womb for these many hours."

Her voice quavered but did not break. "I fear that in truth I carry a male child who, with our men and boys, has ceased to live."

The other women turned stricken faces to her, and Maddon began again to weep. "Not so," she sobbed. "I would have this not be so, my sister. We are suffering enough. Here," she beat against her own full belly with the flat of her hand, "my womb child stirs, and I will it that yours shall, also."

Lystrie looked at the floor. "Would that it were so, dear Madden," she said softly, seeking to console her friend, "but I feel, in truth, that this second son of mine is dead inside my body; and through him, I also shall be stricken."

And so it was that during the night, Lystrie's flesh bloated and changed color to grey and then to purple, and before the sun rose on the final day of Black Winter, she had breathed her last. The other women laid her on the bed that she and Suth had shared in their own home, sang her the Kaddish, and set the cleansing fire.

The days which followed were progressively warmer.

* * *

J'mayya sat in sorrow among the bursting fullness of First Green feeling keenly her own emptiness. Vango is gone, her thoughts fluttered dully, and with him our boy child. /Dowe and Irin and Malee are dead, too. Suth is dead with his son, and Lystrie was poisoned by the dead male child she carried in her womb. Back and forth she rocked the ancient rhythm of mourning, as anguish swelled through her breast and into her throat. And who shall fill us now? How I weep for you, my never child. /Silent tears crept from between her closed lids and sped down her face.

/Be you not troubled, my child of the flesh./ J'mayya felt a sudden sense of presence that was as a wave of compassion which gently sought to comfort and soothe.

/Who?/ J'mayya's thought was edged with fear.

There was a small rippling feeling, a tickling of the spirit, and then, suddenly, J'mayya realized communion.

/All that is of Khaton is likewise of the Mother. I am this, too. My child, what is the cause of your great desolation?/

Now J'mayya felt a gentle probing, then a stirring of Presence, and along with consolation, she received understanding. Her sudden knowledge burst forth in a gasp. "Chromosomes!"

/They do carry the pattern, dear my child, and with some of you the pattern lacked those portions necessary to maintain the body against the feeding spores./ J'mayya received a strong impression of the male sex chromosome, Y-shaped, weak-legged. /Through this open way the spores of the fungus invaded the bodies of the other my children. But those of you who have survived can resist and will breed true./

/But this can not be so, Mother. Khaton has taken the men. Now we will never again be filled and so must cease to be at all./

/Dear my child,/ again J'mayya was comforted, /sleep you beneath the Hylantree and dream well. Indeed, you shall be filled. Let there no longer be a need for mourning./

J'mayya, trusting, went to the Hylantree. As she approached the great plant, she felt a sense of anticipation, and the Hylantree seemed to bend in her direction. She touched the smooth, grey bark of the trunk, ran her hand caressingly over the surface of the wood and felt the pulse of life deep within the tree. Her touch became more intimate; she could feel small knobs and blemishes, marks of the self — the individuality of the organism. As her sense of comfort grew, she impulsively threw her arms about the massive tree trunk in an embrace, pressing her body tightly against the warm wood. A rustle passed through the huge bush of green atop the tree, and branches dipped until the tips of leaves lightly touched against J'mayya's hair. With a small sigh, she lay down at the base of the Hylantree and curled up in a hollow made where a root swelled the ground. There, J'mayya slept, and she dreamed. . . ..

and there is One, and again, there is One, and from these one came more. Every element manifests itself in a multiplicity of shapes, all features of totality. Through the will of the Mother, Khaton is represented in duality through this world and the sisters of the flower. Earth becomes body becomes earth becomes air becomes, again, shifting in forever cycles of is, was, and will be; each itself and more. The creative and receptive patterns of the cosmos whirl together, blend into, from, and between individual functions of expression. All this J'mayya followed through self out to world and on, greater and smaller, and still beyond; until one and many became the Same, and J'mayya was not.

Joy! Sing joy
of leaf and root and bud!
Sing stem, sing seed
dance joy with wind
and praise the world
with leaf and root and bud.

Rise, sap; fall, rain;
grow and ripen, fruit and seed.
Glory! Glory! Cycles follow.
Peaceful, blissful, let it be.
Let it be.

Then J'mayya returned to Identity and journeyed through Learning with her sisters of the flower; and thus from her they knew the sisters of the flesh. When realization had been completed, J'mayya awoke and smiled with the first feeling of a growing secret of which even she was, as yet, unaware.

* * *

Bileya threw up her hands. "Sometimes I feel so futile. We can do only for ourselves. Finala is the last. We will grow old and die, and our daughters will follow us, and who will follow them? We will depart from Khaton in the end, and then there shall be no more."

Maddon pulled her into a tight embrace, and Bileya could feel the flow of strength between them. "We will work well for ourselves. Each of us has her path to follow toward fullness, and endings become beginnings. Fear not, dear Bileya, for all is as it should be, and whatever shall come to pass is right in the eyes of Khaton. It must be so. Indeed, what choice do we have, but that this be so?"

That night, as J'mayya slept in her treetop chamber, she felt a summoning. Swiftly there followed an overwhelming need to communicate with the other women, and suddenly she found that she was calling, broadcasting on a new and different band. She was aware of surprised acknowledgments, recognition from the individual beings of the others—there was Maddon, relaxed even in this new communion, inquisitive. There was Bileya with S'dokay, the latter radiating the slightest trepidation. K'ronna was ready, quiet, waiting to know, and there was even a flicker which was recognizable as tiny Finala, Maddon's infant daughter.

/A time of great happening draws near, my sisters./ J'mayya sensed the questioning of the others and opened herself, permitting the essence of her dreaming with the Hylantree to become known to all who cared to learn. /I can only be certain that through what has passed and what will follow, there will come a growing closer, both with ourselves and one another and all that is Khaton./

J'mayya lay awake for a while, alone. Then she rose and pulled a warm gown over her body. She swept aside a gauzy hanging at one side of her high chamber, stepped over a spread of leaves and into the crotch between two branches, and bent over, wrapping her arms around a third branch. She slid down against the trunk of the tree, found a toehold, grasped a length of rough vine which hung lower down, and slipped to the ground.

The early dawn air was cool with the impending chill that would bring the cycle of fruition to an end and hasten the ripening of seeds. J'mayya tossed her head back and expanded her chest, breathing deeply. She stepped swiftly over the stony ground, almost prancing. She wove deftly in among dew-moist greenery, stooped beneath looping vines and lengths of creeper, and pressed through thornless thickets. She crossed a meadow which rounded the side of a hill and splashed through a stream for a while before she crossed it and continued on her way.

J'mayya walked in a field of tall poles of bandock that were covered with ripening nuts. Absently she pulled a handful of the round seeds and, brushing away the scaly husk, began to chew on the kernels. The triple suns rose higher over the horizon, drawing the heavy dew from ground and leaves into a fine, steamy mist.

J'mayya stopped before a plant which she had never seen before. A profusion of long, red leaves grew thickly on the ground in a rosette, and from the center of this bloomed a giant bud who was just beginning to open. Enormous petals of satin purple with yellow stripes separated slightly at the top of the bud, overlapping, and clinging tightly together toward the bottom.

J'mayya approached the shining blossom, reached out her hand, touched, and felt the bud. A low thrum of energy coursed through the petals, answering J'mayya and also asking. Softly the woman pried one petal away from the others. Gently bending it out from the center, she stooped and peered within, and even knowing, even expecting could not prevent the gasp which said her feelings.

Curled up in the center of the great flower slept an infant girl. A thick bloom of yellow hair covered her head, and her skin was pale violet. A dark purple cord ran from her abdomen to disappear beneath her belly into the heart of the plant, and even as J'mayya watched, the light from the suns shone upon the cord, and it wilted and fell away from the body of the infant.

J'mayya knew, and she reached down, lifted the infant into her arms, held her, and gazed upon her. Feature for feature she was like J'mayya, yet not like; and J'mayya felt a wild exaltation seize through her.

* * *

All blessings, gentle flowers.
Blessings on your welcome fragrance.
Praises for your joyful colors.
May your fertile seeds be many,
Gentle sisters of the flower.
All blessings.

J'mayya sat in a large pocket of soft moss, old, the strength of her body failing. Near her sat two of her five daughters, and close by them rested Bileya, old also, with her children and grandchildren. Maddon was long dead. The other daughters danced about the Hylantree with granddaughters and great-granddaughters, women among flowers, sisters all.

* * *

The shapes of the dancers began to fade, blurred, blended with air and light. There began to swell a masculinity which gradually permeated feeling and being, and Lester came to himself once again.

Consciousness is.

/This, then, was the way of it./ Lester understood now.

/This was the way of it./ The Hylantree remained with him.

/And the women had no sons?/

/They had no sons. Theirs was the only pattern to follow./

/Then are they still able to breed with men?/

/This, my child, I cannot tell you, for I do not know./

Lester was silent a moment. Communication with the Mother remained. Then, /Mother,/ the thought came naturally, /what of us? We are men? What of the black spores? Are they still a threat?/

/If the other leg of the pattern is missing, then when Black Winter comes, the spore fever will strike you./

/Is there nothing we can do to prevent this from happening; to predict the season, perhaps?/

/Dear my child of flesh, these answers I do not have./

Lester was silent again, remembering, recalling portions of his recent experiences to re-examine in the new light of now. /Mother,/ again the feeling of rightness, /what of those of us who seek harmony and do not find it?/

/Then you must sharpen your senses, for harmony is all around you; it only remains for you to be aware of this. Indeed, once you realize that you are more than you may think you are, you will never again settle for less./

/Will you teach me, Mother? Will you accept me as your student?/

/Dear my child! Do you not know that all my children are welcome to me all times and always? No, that you ask shows me you do not. What strange worlds you must come from, that you need question the fact of the totality of your relationship with Khaton, that you are unsure of your welcome. I must reflect on this./ The Presence withdrew.

Lester shivered, looked around. He sat close to a pit of ashes. Amanita squatted nearby, eyes shut, as still as the surrounding boulders. The moons were high in the sky; the lilac moon just beginning to overtake the amber moon. As the two globes moved together, Amanita turned her face up to meet their combined light. She spoke then, lips scarcely moving, "So you will remain, eh Lester? You will stay, and you shall learn."

"So I will," Lester mumbled in reply, not looking at the woman. He tried to stand, but a sudden numbness took his legs, and he fell over. Stiffly, he began to massage his limbs. "It must soon be morning, eh, priest?" he grunted, needing conversation. "I have spent a long night here."

Amanita turned to Lester, ruby eyes wide and shining with reflected moonlight. She laughed softly, the sound deep in her throat. "Indeed, Lester," she purred, "you have spent more than a long night. You dreamed through the day and the next one after, through the night between, as well, and into this one." She rose and went to the long table, returning with a bowl of warm, spicy-smelling liquid. "Drink this," she said gently, placing the bowl in his cold hands. "It will help restore you. Then we shall speak together, and, through words, share knowledge with one another."

4

Korith filled his bowl with fresh chingons stewed in green sauce, then carried his steaming portion over to the wooden bench where Dennivan was eating and sat down next to his friend. Dennivan glanced at Korith, and the corners of his mouth twitched upward, as their gazes locked briefly, then away.

"Pleasant morning." Ganvyla appeared and began to serve herself.

"Pleasant morning to you," Dennivan mumbled around a mouthful of stew, while Korith looked up at the woman and smiled his friendship. Both men wore tunics of soft fabric — Korith's of bright blue trimmed with tiny white embroidered leaves and belted with a thick band of purple, Dennivan's of a yellow which was a shade darker than his hair, bordered and belted with a nappy, black material. Both men wore their new clothing comfortably; their old uniforms were as comfortably folded away in a corner of their chamber.

Dennivan stood up and took his mug from the ground. His hand brushed Korith's knee. "Can I get you some guara?" he offered.

Korith smiled, his eyes on Dennivan's face. "Thanks. My cup is near the pitcher." He looked away, still smiling.

Dennivan filled the two mugs with hot green liquid. "Ganvyla?" He held one out to the woman.

Ganvyla swallowed a bite of stew. "Thank you, Dennivan. I have mine." She lifted her cup, showing him, then continued with her meal.

Dennivan brought the guara over to Korith and handed a mug to the other man, touching their fingers together for an instant. He sat down, sipped his hot drink, then addressed Ganvyla: "Is Pahma?"

"Pahma has gone." The woman continued to eat.

"Gone?" Korith looked up, startled. "Where?"

"To other places, other events."

"And she will return . . . ?" Dennivan asked, waiting to hear when.

Ganvyla shrugged. She wiped out her bowl with a piece of soft roll, set the bowl on the ground, and chewed the bread softly. "Who can say?" she replied cryptically. "When one is free to flow, one can go and return and welcome. She will return when she is here—perhaps before next season, perhaps after many seasons."

"She *will* return?" Dennivan voiced his concern.

"We are special sisters," Ganvyla replied.

"But why has she gone? Why then does she not remain with you?"

Ganvyla looked at the men curiously. "But surely even among your sisters of many worlds each person is blessed with her own path to follow. Some of us may find that our ways flow together for their greatest portions, yet we each find those bypasses which we must take alone, as ultimately we each remain alone. So, now, Pahma wishes to do that, and I wish to do this. We will follow our desires separately, loving each other throughout."

"But don't you mind?"

"Mind?"

"She is who you love. She is away."

Ganvyla shook her head. "Strange one, you speak as though love depends on physical presence, as though love ceases with separation. Love will not be so restricted—it flows as a fresh spring from our earth-center; from us, through us, and around us, until we become earth-center."

"But she has gone—she who you love. She does not wish to be with you. Does this fact not cause you grief?"

Ganvyla was quiet for a while, looking from Korith to Dennivan, back and forth. "Dear sisters," she spoke soberly, "are your worlds truly so strange? Does it follow, where you come from, that departure is is considered a rejection? Indeed, Pahma and myself might each prefer to be here together, but there are other things to do, and choices need be made. She will return when she does return, and if by chance or plan all returns have ended, I shall accept this."

"Well," said Korith, putting his dish down on the ground beside him, "I really don't understand at all." He sat back, moving so that his shoulder and arm rested their length against the arm and shoulder of Dennivan.

Dennivan glanced at Korith and leaned slightly into the contact. "However," he said, "whether we understand or not is far from a matter of urgency. We are here, now, and there are things to be done."

5

Captain Eliat lay on his back on his mat in his chamber staring up at his ceiling, eyes burning from lack of moisture. The canopy over his head was crossed with shadows, as the light from the moons played among the treetops outside. Robwill had been good to him, the Captain thought, supportive, almost waiting on him with eagerness to help. Still, the concern the younger man showed for him made the Captain feel all the more keenly his responsibility to the other men in his charge on this mission. He was a Captain, a United Planetary Explorer, and that meant he was Responsible. He had not done well. Already he had lost . . . no, don't think about that . . . but it was an undeniable fact and had to be faced . . . four crew! He had lost four people on three planets, and a fifth man lost a portion of his body on still another mission. Now five more of his crew could not be reached. He would not lose them, too. He would find them, locate them, and remove them from the madness of this planet of beastly females. He sighed loudly and flung an arm across his eyes. It was all the fault of that woman Amaranth who was the one in charge. No doubt she had put her women up to capturing the men. Perhaps she had imprisoned them. Perhaps she had even . . . but no, don't think about that, either. Don't have fantasies over what may not be the case in fact. Do not even consider the future except in terms of positive action. In the morning, resolved the Captain, he would go to Amaranth, demand to see her if necessary, and then force her to return his men to him.

Plans circled through Captain Eliat's dimming awareness, resolution coloring the shades of his dream:

Captain Eliat screamed, feeling jagged crystal edges suddenly slice into his body, severing muscle and tendon, breaking bone and cutting through the flesh beyond. He felt the swift rush of fluids flow out of him. He felt the scream in his brain of severed nerve tissue warning of imminent destruction of the organism. The pain, excruciating as it was, still was as nothing next to the agonizing knowledge that he was going to die here, alone, on a strange world, without even a home left behind to feel his absence.

With a rush, he ascended swiftly, swooping away from one consciousness to another. He peered out of the window of the copter. The slime that covered the sea below them was grey streaked with mucousy flecks of red and yellow. Bubbles dotted the surface of the slime, and every few moments, some of them would burst, allowing a seepage of brownish fluid that was soon covered over again by the grey ooze. He stared intently at the sea, as Arboth, who was flying the copter, brought the machine down lower. "Do you see something moving?" he murmured to his partner.

Captain Eliat scrutinized the surface beneath them. Yes, he did think that perhaps there was something . . . Then he cried out, as horror broke from the glutinous mess below. A huge, gaping maw filled with grey, spongelike substance emerged from the sea, great pores in the sponge opening and closing in independent greedy sucking, spewing forth clots of slime. Both of them were thrown from their seats, safety straps bursting from the strain of movement, as the copter was torn from the air by great tentacles which rose from the ocean. Yet, merciless awareness remained with the Captain, and his staring eyes recorded image by image the dreadful events that followed; as the gross creature tugged the copter beneath the mucousy surface into brown and evil fluid, until its sucking orifices applied to the glass windows broke through, and oblivion entered.

He felt a sudden heat against his feet, and then agony seared up his legs to the knees. He stood in soft sand which ate through boot and fabric to burn into his flesh like some insidious acid. Slowly, inexorably, he felt the line of pain etch higher, and his thoughts exploded with panic at the realization that he was in fact sinking deeper into the burning sand; that it was swallowing him, even as it burned the flesh from his bones. He saw the faces of his friends and crewmates frozen in dismay, as they watched him founder from their safety of more stable land, unable to help him. Then pain released him from awareness.

Captain Eliat looked down. Close to his boot sat a small, green lizard. "Ech!" The Captain recoiled, heavy foot automatically striking out to crush life and breath in blood from the emerald creature. Captain Eliat ground his boot against the corpse, mixing flesh and bone with dirt and gravel until both were unrecognizable as either one or the other.

A sudden carrion stench erupted from the ruined heap. Captain Eliat stepped back, gagging. A ringing in his ears grew into a buzzing, then a roar of vibration; and the air moved in gusts from the pressure of wings, as scores of giant flies came to the smell. The Captain backed away, avoiding the insects, trying not to cross the place where their passing left the air striped with threads of foul vibration. He turned and trotted toward the coastline. He followed the water, keeping to the bank even though he often had to detour around thickets which blocked his path. He rounded the base of a wide plateau, and there was a small open craft pulled up on the bank of the lake.

Captain Eliat pushed the boat free and clambered aboard. Stepping the length of the vessel, he freed the rudder from its moorings, then pulled a heavy waterproof slicker and wide-brimmed hat on as protection against the heavy wind which sprang up, blowing storm clouds to crowd together overhead. The air grew cold and damp, mist hanging heavy against his skin. The Captain sat in the stern of the open boat, steering hard against high waves which battered the sides of the craft. The boat lifted above the water, and Seal held to the edge, feeling the helplessness and lack of control that came of being Passenger. Seal stared at the heavy swells of water, icy grey blending with the fog until it was no longer possible to determine where the two became separate. Suddenly Seal rose, dove over the edge of the boat, and the Captain pulled the rudder hard to keep the small vessel steady and close by. Seal swam beneath the water, surfaced, and threw the Captain a sardine.

Captain Eliat tucked the small fish inside his leather jerkin and set out on his way to seek a kind cook with a warm kitchen. His feet beat a tattoo against the hard, dirt road in time to the jolly tune which ran through his head until it found a way out of his mouth in a merry whistle. Thus he danced over the fields and through the woods, across a stone arc footbridge which spanned a deep brook, and up to the door of the castle which stood atop the hill. He reached out, grasped the heavy handle of the door firmly, and pulled the great door open.

There before him was a narrow chimney leading up. Captain Eliat stepped into the shaft, and the door slammed shut behind him, sealing him in. A cold fury began to grow in his gut at the thought of his being tricked and trapped. He searched the walls for a possible portal of release. At last, satisfied that there was no way for movement save the shaft itself, he braced his back against one portion, set his feet against the opposite wall, and slowly began to inch his way upward.

He rose higher and higher still, until perspective brought the walls of the well to a point when he looked below him. He wondered at the source of light — surely by all reason the shaft should be dark; there was no circle of light or any other reflection to indicate an exit at the top. As a matter of fact, the Captain noticed, as he looked up, pausing for a moment in his climb, that the upper portion of the walls likewise vanished into a point, so far and high did they rise above him. Yet, there was nothing to do but push and slide, inch by inch, ever onward and upward.

His back began to ache where muscles protested the constant movement and extreme pressure, and his skin smarted where his clothing had worn through and the grey rock rubbed him. His legs cramped, as did his arms which were outstretched, pressed against the walls, spreadeagled for added support. He felt the shaft beneath him as a great, yawning gap, felt the pull of air almost as though a vacuum were being created by his ascent to pull him down again as soon as he ascended high enough to give it strength. He began to despair of ever reaching the top, if in fact there *were* a top, an exit, a way out. His legs quivered, and he sensed the distance he would fall if he were to relax his hold even the slightest, relieve the unbearable strain and pressure for even one moment. He braced his body even more strongly against the walls of the shaft, forcing himself to press outward and hold, no longer master of his body enough to push it to further action. Yet he strove upward, willing his very cells to pull towards the top where there must, at last, be exit.

The grey stone floor of the kitchen vomited him forth, and he came to his feet beside an urn.

"So," the cook said, approaching him and taking his hand, "you have arrived. We have waited long for you." The cook kissed the backs of his fingers, then returned to tend the fire. Singly, from different areas of the kitchen, the lesser cooks approached the Captain, each repeating the ritual. Over their bent heads, the Captain surveyed the great room. It was completely bare of furnishings and utensils, and no sweet herbs hung drying from the rafters. A huge fire dominated the center of the kitchen. The Captain squinted at the fire, then recoiled at the sight of formless creatures caught in cages around the blaze, skin crisped from the constant heat. They had no more strength than to hang against the bars and moan feebly, no strength to beat even one demand for freedom.

The cook approached Captain Eliat again, pressed closely and seductively against him, ran searching fingers inside the front of his vest, touch fluttering in exploration against his chest. The cook slowly drew forth the tiny fish and carried it reverently to the fire, placing it in a round pan over the flames. Expertly the cook turned the fish, browning it evenly on both sides, then slid it onto a crystal platter and carried it to the Captain, offering it to him. The lesser cooks joined hands in a ring around the duo, and as Captain Eliat took the platter from the hands of the cook, they chorused, "Remember, one sardine does not a seafood dinner make!"

6

Side by side, Prechard and Camas pulped succulence fruit in a great vat, while with them worked women and girls, singing, talking, hands in thick orange pulp and juice up the the elbows. Sweet fruity fingers found their way to mouths from time to time, while sticky liquid dripped onto cloth, flesh, and ground. The fruit was cool against sun-warmed skins, pressed delightfully between working fingers; soft, juicy fruit-meat coming apart from around the smooth, marble-sized balls that contained the seeds.

The vat was built over a large pit in the midst of a succulence thicket. It was a simple matter to pluck the ripe fruit from the shrubs and toss them into the huge cistern. After the vat was filled and the fruit pulped, a fire was kindled in the pit, and the mixture cooked until it frothed. Then a ferment was added, and the vat was capped. When the fermentation stopped and the residue settled to the bottom, the liquor was considered matured, the vat was opened, and each woman came to take a portion.

Prechard was working automatically, mind-tripping, when suddenly, without warning, Camas lifted a handful of the cool, wet, pulpy fruit and flung it at her. It struck the side of her head and dripped down her face and neck and into the front of her tunic. Laughing, Camas kissed her on the mouth through rivulets of juice, then leaped into the surrounding succulence plants and through.

Prechard gave chase, dashed through the soft shrubs heavy with orange fruit and out onto a grassy slope that was covered with creeping vines that bore white, trumpet-shaped flowers along their lengths. She passed beneath a fruiting sorchew tree, searching for a glimpse of ebony skin, when, with an explosion of new laughter, Camas leaped upon her from behind the sorchew and bore her to the ground.

Camas and Prechard rolled over the white flowers which gave forth a heady fragrance as they were crushed. Then Camas tore loose and scrambled deftly to her feet. She dodged behind a sapling, then ran swiftly down the grassy bank towards the pond at the bottom, stripping her tunic over her head as she went. Tossing her clothing onto the bank, she dove smoothly into the water.

Prechard flew down the bank in chase. She dropped her own tunic beside that of Camas and splashed into the pond, breath exploding in a flurry of bubbles, as she stepped into a deep spot and her head went under water. She saw a dark foot, grabbed at it, and missed. By the time she surfaced and shook hair and water out of her eyes, Camas had scrambled nimbly out of the pond and was perched on a stony overhang. She regarded Prechard quizzically for a moment, and Prechard saw herself mirrored in silver eyes. Then her reflection burst into a glowing shower, as Camas broke into laughter.

They lay in the grass to dry and warm themselves, and they talked, enjoying the closeness. Prechard was grateful for the time alone with Camas. Her courage rose, and she wanted to be honest about her own needs. "What I find difficult to understand," she said at last, "and especially hard to accept, is the ease with which you move in your relationships from one to the other."

"What is there to understand or accept?" Camas asked. "I do what I do. You do what you do. I am here, now; you are here, now."

"But what about later?" Prechard struggled with the words.

"What about tomorrow? What if I turn to you and you are not there but are with someone else?" she voiced her fear.

"If you were truly here, now, Prechard," Camas replied, "you would not dwell on images of what has passed or fantasies of what might be."

Prechard pressed her fingernails against her knees and watched the little crescent marks they made in her flesh. "I grow more than fond of you, Camas. I have need for you. When you spread yourself among so many others, you diminish yourself. If you give all of you to others, then what will be left for me?"

"Dear, strange Prechard," Camas' voice was soft, "you speak as if it were necessary to take from one in order to give to another. This is not the way of it. Loving has no bounds, no limits of being."

Prechard felt anger at the difference between them. "On my world this is not the case, and I find your way difficult to comprehend. On my world we are matched one to one by the State, and this is our security. We each have our destined other to help us define who we are, and because we are assigned in this manner to one another for the duration of our lifetimes, we do not need to be watchful of the other out of fear that we may lose to another this one to whom we are mated and be left forever after with nothing."

"Well, I don't know about the left with nothing part—for after all, you do have your self—but the rest of what you say, although I may not wholly agree, is not entirely beyond my understanding." Camas turned from her belly onto her back. "How else can we really perceive ourselves, after all, except by means of our reflection in others and our effect on our world? And we must relate in some manner with another person, for in the process of continuing to define ourself to another, we define ourself to ourself."

Prechard dug her fingers into the soft soil beneath the grass. "Where I come from, my friend, we have no other means of definition than this; and since life itself is never sure, we forever fear the loss of our mate to death. Because we are the only means of security to the being of one another, we fear this loss over all things. In our desperation, we clutch at each other, hanging on with all our strength, and the result is that we strangle one another, we choke each other to death while we still live."

"How does the State then decide how to match you, two by two,

two by two, in this manner for the duration of your lives? Are you happy this way?"

"I do not know. The State decides. We follow as we are assigned. Happiness is not a consideration."

Camas chewed on a piece of grass. "On Khaton, each has her own course in life to follow," she said thoughtfully. "With some of us, our paths may flow together for many years. With others, we may cross ways but briefly. Some we simply pass, and some we never meet. So it goes. Still," she stretched, arched her back, "worlds are different from one to the other, and even among worlds there are differences. Where there are differences, however, there are also similarities. So come, now, sister of my heart, the suns are sinking low, and there is a special place I wish to show you for the rising of the moons." She rose, picked up her fruit-stained tunic and pulled it on, then held out her hand to Prechard.

7

"Follow!" called Arum. She grabbed a low-hanging length of creeping vine, took a running start along the ground, leaped, pulled, and swung herself up onto the widest branch of the picado tree.

"Coming," called Delfan in reply. She caught the long vine, as Arum released it, allowing it to swing back. She ran, thrust with her feet hard against the ground, swung her legs forward and reached before her with toes straining for clearance. She saw the branch pass her, swift blur of Arum's face smiled at her, and then she felt the closeness of wood and flung her right leg ahead, out, and over the anchorage of a smaller branch that angled up from the wide branch where Arum perched. She flung the vine back and caught the branch with her hands, feeling rough bark warm her palms, calling down over her shoulder, "Follow!"

Allium caught the vine and swung into the tree, light body seeming to float through the air like a streak of copper flecked with red, trailing yellow hair. She sat with her sisters, three friends searching for the next point of movement with no contest in mind. Allium stood up, balanced on the limb of the picado. "Follow!" she announced. She scurried along the branch to an elbow where a tangle of twigs fanned out grown with close red leaves. She bounced onto the nest of twigs, and the branch bent slightly, springing back to thrust her up and out. She sailed through the air and came to land precisely where she had planned to in the center of a thicket of cushiony, resilient powta plants.There was a thump near her, then another, as Arum and Delfan followed in turn, each girl placing her body in flight to land in a desired spot.

"Follow!" gasped Delfan, a little out-of-breath from her trip. She burrowed down through the spongy leaves to the ground where, on hands and knees, she tunneled a way out of the powta thicket. Arum and Allium followed close behind, bursting from the growth almost simultaneously.

"Follow!" shrieked Allium, and the three girls in line raced across a field of green and gold-flecked grain, young bodies running strong amid the ripening fruit.

"Follow!" exploded Arum. She stepped into a brook and waded upstream, Delfan and Allium behind her, until they reached the rocky pool and spring which was its source.

"Follow," laughed Delfan. She stripped her tunic over her head, threw it onto orange boulders away from the pool, and submerged her body in the clear water.

Later, the girls lay together atop a large boulder. Delfan, round, brown-skinned, yellow hair in a thick braid wound about her head like a crown, closed green eyes and turned her face to the light from the suns. Arum's naked flesh shone white against the brilliant orange stone, face nesting in a halo of apricot hair. She turned her head so that her cheek rested against the back of Delfan's hand, feeling comfort in the warmth of skin touching together. Allium sat with her knees drawn up under her chin, hands clasped together about her legs, watching the flow of sparkling water as it bubbled from the cleft in the rocks and fed into the deep pool. The three were together quietly in communion with one another and with all Khaton, until they could no longer bear the beauty in their need for celebration.

Allium stood up. "I," she announced, "will be priest."

"And I will be helper," volunteered Delfan.

"And I will be the people," said Arum with the satisfaction of completion.

The girls scrambled for their tunics, but then Delfan held out her arms to stop them. "If we are going to have a ceremony," she said seriously, "we should at least make ourselves proper robes."

"Yes!" Allium shouted her enthusiasm of agreement. "And an altar." She began gathering stones from around the pool and heaping them together.

Arum brought handfuls of harvest flowers, roots well packed with dirt, and placed them in large spaces between the stones so that they would continue to grow there even after the children had finished their games and departed.

They completed the altar, edging it around with chips of the bright orange stone, and then began to look for material to make robes. Allium pulled a loose piece of velinska bark free from the trunk of the tall tree. "This will make a fine priest's robe," she called to the others. The thin material folded over in her hands, and she used her teeth to worry a small hole in the bark near the middle of the fold. She pushed both her thumbs through the rent and carefully tore an opening large enough to put her head through. She gathered the sides together, and Arum pinned them with iridescent orange slivers which she had picked up from the bottom of the pool during her swim.

"Here," called Delfan from a hill above the spring. Arum and Allium raced up the slope to where their friend stood. "This will make a splendid helper's robe!" She held out several portions of dried lufamoss. Arum and Allium worked together to wind the moss about Delfan's ample form, tucking one piece into another and bringing a corner over one round shoulder before fastening the fabric. Then all three girls gathered flowers and stuck them through the spaces between the fibers of the moss, until it was easy to pretend that Delfan wore a gown made completely from flowers.

"I can just wear my tunic to be the people," said Arum.

"With garlands for the ceremony, don't forget," added Delfan. Swift fingers wove chains of more flowers to loop about Arum's head and over her shoulders.

Allium clapped her hands in glee. "All blessings!" she sang. "I think we look so beautiful, wonderful sisters! Now let's go find a chalice, and then we can do our ceremony."

"Will we want one of stone?" Delfan asked.

"Or wood?" Arum considered.

"Or even a leaf will do." Allium gave a little skip and joined hands with the other girls, and the three of them frolicked down the hill.

"Maybe here . . ." Delfan broke away from the group and ran toward an open bed of jadestone. She bent over the tumbled rocks, searching for a stone to serve as a chalice. Her hand went out toward a possible form, and then she heard a terrible sound, the moan, a low sound squeezed forth almost as breath, no life of feeling behind it. Delfan looked around her. The moan sounded again, rasping, rattling. She tracked the noise to a calama sapling, and there at the base sat Danal, propped against the thin trunk, head leaning to one side. His eyes stared, glassy, blind, and spittle dripped from his slack lips and ran down into old, crusted froth which caked his beard.

Delfan ran over to him. "Strange sister," she spoke urgently, voice low, "can I help you in your need?" Breath moaned in and out of his chest through his mouth and throat. "She is bent!" Delfan whispered to herself. She reached down and took Danal's hands, one in each of hers. "Come, bent sister, and we will find help." She stepped back, still holding, and Danal rose and moved to her.

Arum and Allium came running towards them. "What, Delfan?" called the younger girl.

"Sh," Delfan muttered. "Can't you see? She is bent."

"Oooooh." Arum and Allium slowed, tiptoed up to Delfan and Danal, looked curiously at the pair. "She is the strange sister,"Arum said in awe. "What has taken her, Delfan?"

"I don't know." Delfan tugged gently at Danal's hands, and he came easily with her. "But one thing is certain and that is we must bring her to Wyoleth as quickly as we can."

Arum and Allium nodded, eyes large.

Delfan released one of Danal's hands and stepped towards the path which would take them to Wyoleth. Danal moved with her, and Arum and Allium followed behind.

8

"What have you done with my crew?" Captain Eliat strode angrily into Amaranth's chambers. He paced about, not looking at the woman who sat erect on a high backed stone chair, hands resting on armrests carved with delicate flowers.

"Done?" She regarded him cooly, her question plain, yet saying no more words for him to grasp.

"I have lost communication." The Captain's anger began to build. "I have had no contact with five of my crew — Lester, Danal, Prechard, Korith, and Dennivan — in these many days. And I do not even know how many days it has been!" He spun about and marched over to stand before Amaranth, hands on hips, glaring into her face. "I will confront you now, Amaranth, and demand that you tell me what you have done with my people!"

Amaranth leaned back, her amusement plain. "So you are still demanding, Captain Eliat," she said. "Have you not yet discovered that there are other ways of making your wishes known?"

"Do you not deny, then, that you have taken my crew?" the Captain persisted, leaning closer to Amaranth.

Amaranth stood up and walked away from the man. "Your problem, Captain Eliat," she said, "is that you seem to have too many fantasies of the way that things really are not. You come rushing into my chambers, disturbing my meditation, with all your preconceived ideas of circumstances which you do not know, and you are so closed up with your lack of perception that you are unable to see what actually is before you. Thus, you make inappropriate noises and gestures and drown out any attempt that another being will make to try to indicate to you these facts. You hear the currents of the ether and think it is a hurricane carrying a message for your ears alone. How can you take responsibility for your sisters when you do not relate with them and thus cannot know them, their selves and their needs? How can you make reliable judgments as to what is, Captain Eliat, when your mind is so full of forms of your own invention?"

Captain Eliat turned, rigid, faced Amaranth, and spoke stiffly, "You mistake my communication. You have not understood my words. I am quite well able to draw logical conclusions from information which my senses provide—information which is correctly relayed from what is to what I think is. My sense of order is perfect, as is my understanding of events which follow in sequence. I am a Captain. My perception of cause and effect is perfect to the point of prediction. I repeat, Amaranth, I am a Captain. I am a Captain, and you make a mockery of me. Your women have seduced away my crew, even as you have seduced away my reason!"

"I?" Amaranth observed the man curiously, her head tilted slightly to one side. "I have done nothing, Captain Eliat, except be. You seek to use me as a mirror for the causes of your own shortcomings; but look you well, Captain Eliat, my glass is clear. I am I. Do not attempt to find within me only what you wish or to bend me to fit your fantasies of me. Because I am aware that you do this, such attempts on your part will be futile." She turned and glided over to a table where she busied herself with lighting a censer. "Indeed, how do you keep in contact with one another, Captain Eliat?" She glanced at the man. "Even I can tell you that three of the strangers have been working well with our sisters of Khaton, and two of them are, in truth, special sisters. Another learns with the priest. Of the last, I know not, nor do I care." She swung the censer, and smoke billowed out in great clouds. "If you wished to summon your people and could not make contact with them, if you needed assistance, all you had to do was to make your desire known. So, now I shall tell you that the four strange ones of whom I know the whereabouts will soon be aware of your need for them, and you may wait for them to arrive at your chambers. Good morning, Captain Eliat, you had best go to meet them."

Captain Eliat eyed the smoke suspiciously, moving away as it spread in the air. "So, you do know where they are, then," he said, his voice hard. "It is as I suspected. In truth you have taken my crew and so, you shall return them. I will save them from you—I, their Captain. You shall not make of us whatever you have done to your own men." He turned and stalked through the doorway.

9

Danal frothed and sputtered, as Wyoleth held a shallow cup to his lips. He sat on a low bench in a leafy chamber, rigid, empty-eyed, the foam of his madness on his beard. The woman knelt next to him, trying to spill some liquid into his mouth. "Here, now, poor bent sister. What guilt must you carry to have twisted you in this way? What fear binds you?" She tipped the cup, and a yellow fluid splashed across his tongue and dribbled over his jaw and down his neck. He swallowed convulsively, gulping, then clamped his lips tightly together. Wyoleth smiled. "That will do you good." She stroked his hands. "Come back, poor creature. Truly the here and now could not hold such terrors as you imagine. There is no threat in this place save those phantoms of your own making; and they, as such, can be undone only by you."

Wyoleth turned to the three girls. "Where did you find her?"

"Delfan saw her first," said Allium, nodding towards her friend.

The older girl turned serious green eyes to the woman. "The strange one was sitting on the ground all huddled up against a calama sapling. I heard her moan, and I went to see if she needed aid."

"The strange sister didn't speak at all," Arum interjected. "Delfan stood before her and asked her need, and the strange one did not reply, nor did she look to Delfan."

"She was bent," muttered Delfan. "Bent sisters cannot."

"So Delfan reached to her and took her hand," Arum continued, glancing respectfully from Wyoleth to Danal and back to Delfan, "and the bent sister stood and came away with us."

"She seemed so light," Delfan murmured. "She took my hand in so slight a hold that I could barely feel her flesh against mine. She made no resistance; she rose from the ground as if she were a Zooner pod whose mooring had come loose and was lifting on the wind. We brought her to you, and it seemed that she floated, hollow, needing only to be guided by my most delicate touch. I felt as though I must take care not to push her this way and that, lest she lose her grasp and drift away."

"You did right to bring her here," Wyoleth said. "She is badly bent; she is twisted away from her present being in actuality. We must work together to call her back to the world of here and now."

Wyoleth moved across the chamber. She placed three huge candles triangularly about the bench where Danal was sitting. "Here, now, dear sisters," she seated one girl behind each candle, "we must link together firmly. We must bind our selves about the bent sister and form a mesh to give her support. Then, holding her in this manner, we can sustain her in her search for her way back. We can help her to lead herself to the present of no threat." Wyoleth stood before Danal in the center of the triangle. She held his hands one in each of her own, and she began to sing to him, soft song sounding in joyful invitation, singing to him.

The girls closed their eyes and blended their melodies to lift through the tones of Wyoleth, singly and together in different complexities of progressions, restating the theme in simplification, singing to him. They sent their selves to twine together through their song, growing from Khaton to a splendid web of energy, an entity which sent forth threadlets of being to search for one who has been lost to self, calling to all of she who is bent away from herself and therefore Khaton, seeking to heal and to bring once again to wholeness.

Vibrations of call wound through lost and lonely places, filled spaces with the flow before draining away to other cosmic capillaries. Singing to him, the tune sounded as a beacon to bring him back to being. From far away, there came a flicker of response, a subtle recognition from that which once had been Danal and now was twisted and torn. " . . . I . . ." sought to bridge the distance with the faintest of echoes in answer, and the song swelled, inviting to celebration this tiny broadcasting of awareness, luring forth realization with promises of growth.

Then the summons came as the clanging of a great gong, and all unity was shattered.

10

"What, Lester, do you fear?" Amanita stared at him, holding his see with her own. The light from the triple suns brought tones of peach to the pink of her hair and an orange glow to her ruby eyes.

Lester glanced away, looked at the ground, held to the shimmering of tiny heat waves above the bare dirt and stone. "I fear, priest. I do fear. I will not try to fool you by hiding my fear. I am terribly afraid, and fear is ever present in my gut. I fear death. I fear to be alone. I fear loss, and I fear oblivion. I fear all which I do not know. I fear all that I cannot control. I fear to be, and I fear the end to all things. Most of all, priest, I fear to be forever afraid."

"And can you in truth fear to be alone even knowing that we each remain alone and so are not alone? Can you fear death even with the knowledge that you are more than life or death? How can you fear the Source, if you remember that in truth you are the Source? Lester, your fears make no sense."

"Then even what this comes down to is that I fear pain. I fear to hurt. I fear to suffer."

Amanita rose and walked over to the long table, busying her hands with small tasks. She glanced around at Lester who sat silently watching her. She spoke to him slowly, giving each word its time. "Before Union can be complete, Lester, you must become Union. There can be no separation. Pain is nothing more than a transition, a time of change, a brief interlude. Indeed, pain and the other face of pain which is pleasure are each all that is not the other; still, they both imply and contain the other, and each can in actuality be that which it is not. Only when you are able to accept your pain will it cease to hurt you; for pain is born of conflict, and with complete acceptance comes an end to all suffering."

Lester looked up at the priest, head tilted back, chin high. His voice sounded hard and flat. "This is the way with us, priest. This is fact, and it is the way of men that fear is a part of us and is common to all mankind. Although it often may be said, 'There goes a man without fear', this is not true, nor can it be, for fear is a part of all men. Better let it be said, 'There goes a man who has conquered his fear, that he is not ruled by it.'. This is what I strive for. I shall face my fear and fight my fear, and I will win or lose. This is the way of man."

Amanita held his gaze with her own, seeing deep through pink into his soul and wondering at the conflict. "There are other ways," she pointed out. "As long as you fight your fear, you will suffer the pain that is born of resistance and which you must further fight, in turn, only to breed more pain." She chuckled, a deep sound far back in her throat. "When you accept your fear and that which you fear along with it, there comes an end to conflict, and behold, you have won." Amanita paused for a moment out of conversation. She looked away, expression one of expectation, hesitated, then turned to Lester again. "I have received a calling—a summons from Amaranth calling all strangers in behalf of the Captain to return to their chambers at once."

Lester slapped his forehead. "I forgot!" he exploded. "I forgot about reporting in and maintaining contact and all our rules of conduct while on exploration. I must have been gone for days and days, so taken have I been with you, priest, and your doings. What madness! I have not even communicated with my companions nor reported to my Captain. What breaches of discipline!" He stood up and laughed loudly, body shaking with release of tension. "Madness," he repeated, "and madness. So, for all that, I feel not the least bit ashamed or that I must repent of my actions. Still," he turned, wiped tears from his eyes, breathed deeply until shudders subsided, "I shall respond appropriately and return with my report. Good-bye, priest." Impulsively, he reached out to her, held her pale hands for a moment pressed gently with his own. "I should like to return here, if such a journey is possible, and if I may."

Amanita freed her hands from his grasp. Her mouth twitched slightly at the corners. "So you may, Lester," she answered him, "and if you must, then so you will."

11

"You realize, of course," Captain Eliat paced back and forth in the clearing, "that this Amaranth and her assorted women have been manipulating us." He gestured with his hands. "I have read tales of ensorcellment, but I always thought them fictions. Now I fear that I will have no weapons to fight. Eh, Robwill?"

Robwill sat on a flat stone nearby, pretending not to notice his captain's strange behaviors. He looked up, fixed his gaze on the distant trees. "Sir . . ." his response was neither question nor statement.

The Captain spun about and strode over to stand before the younger man. His eyes narrowed, and a small tic started at one corner of his mouth. "It doesn't matter, of course," he said coldly, "whether or not you understand. The fact is that I am aware of the problems we are facing, and as Your Captain, I have a responsibility for the well-being and safety of all who are in my charge." His face fell suddenly. Slow tears started at the corners of his eyes, and he sighed deeply, a hollow sound, empty. "I can no longer avoid the issues of importance. The fact of the matter is that I have sorely failed this responsibility in the past." He straightened, and his voice hardened along with his expression. "I shall not fail again. I will lose none of you who remain the way I lost poor Kedrick, Juna and Arboth, and Wallaway . . ." he choked on the last name, and his tic worsened.

"But, sir," Robwill was quick to interject, "none of that was of your doing. They were accidents, could have happened to anyone, anywhere."

Captain Eliat drew himself up until he stood tall, shoulders pressed back. "I am Captain," he reminded the other man, "and I am, in fact, Responsible. I shall not allow another Incident. I will, at all costs, Protect the men remaining in my charge." His eyes gleamed, and Robwill drew back. Captain Eliat stared past him, over his shoulder. The Captain's throat convulsed. "What? What?" he choked.

Robwill spun about. A woman had entered the clearing. A woman? No, it was . . . Dennivan? Dennivan. Dennivan was back. Robwill blinked. His crewmate was wearing a tunic of iridescent mauve which came to mid-thigh where it was hung with a fine, bright yellow fringe. These same yellow threads were worked intricately into the weave of the bell-shaped sleeves. The tunic was tied at the waist with a thick, black cord. Black, wide-toed boots reached halfway up Dennivan's calves where they flared out, the tops folded over and set with small shining stones of yellow and purple. A nappy mauve headband covered his forehead and held back his fluff of hair.

Captain Eliat's eyes widened, then narrowed into slits. His nostrils flared, his lips drew together, and a flush rose from his neck and spread over his face. "Would you mind," his voice came tightly from between clenched teeth, "explaining the meaning of this exhibition?"

"Sir?" Dennivan half-smiled.

"Why are you dressed in this disgusting, outrageous manner? How dare you? Where is your uniform?" The Captain's voice shook with fury.

Dennivan drew back, annoyed rather than intimidated. "My uniform, sir," he said coldly, "is in the chamber where I have been staying, this which I wear being better suited for my involvements and also to my taste. I came in haste to answer your summons which interrupted me at my work, and I did not take the time to change my clothing, since I did not feel that it was necessary."

"You did not feel that it was necessary," mocked the Captain. "You have no idea what has been happening here. You are being used, and you remain ignorant. What kind of work have you been doing, that you return to show your crewmates that you have become like a woman of this accursed planet?"

Dennivan flushed and half turned away, his composure shaken by an old and still unrecognized shame. He breathed deeply before he replied. "I have been learning of the people, as we were instructed to do. I have been following my orders, even as has my crewmate Korith. Together we have been learning of the people and working with them, and they say we are no mean helpmates."

"So where is Korith now?" Captain Eliat held his advantage.

"We were, the two of us together, working with the women

among the Toolas when your summons came. Korith remains to assist, since the task of cutting requires many hands. I came, and I will return to Korith with information and your orders, or he will come here when his work has been completed."

"He is to come here now." The Captain's command was curt. "Go and get him. And take off that disgraceful skirt before you return to be among men. I wish to see you next in proper uniform and with a proper attitude." He turned away. Orders had been given.

12

Lester continued on the track which led him away from the caverns of Amanita and toward the chambers of the crew. Everything around him seemed to swell with a new vibrancy; everything fairly hummed with life and with meaning. He plucked a purpleskinned fruit from a vine as he passed, admired its brilliance in the light from the suns, then put it to his mouth, embraced the shining globule with his lips, crushed it between his teeth, and swallowed, swallowed, swallowed. He gloried in the feel of cool air against his skin and breathed deeply, drawing in the life energy of Khaton. He stopped and squatted before a small shrub that still bore a few late blossoms, touched one soft, pink bloom with his forefinger, then stood up again and continued on his way.

"Lester!" His solitary pleasure was interrupted by the sound of a voice from behind him. He turned to see a woman of Khaton . . . no, it was his crewmate dressed like a woman of Khaton. He blinked.

"Prechard?"

"I." She was wearing a violet tunic clasped with a tight silver sash and embroidered closely with grey leaves above the waist. On her feet were supple-looking silver boots that came just above her ankles, and tiny purple chillblooms were stuck into her wooly yellow hair. She looked very beautiful. She stopped, seeming to see herself reflected in the expression of her crewmate. She looked down. "Oh," she laughed, "I must present quite a sight to you out of uniform, but Camas told me that there was a summons and I had best make haste. I had not been in touch with the crew for days, so I thought I had better be on my way. My uniform was at least a day's journey from where I was, so I came as I was dressed. Besides," she shrugged her shoulders, "these clothes are much more comfortable. I feel quite at home in them. Here, feel there," she held a foot up for Lester to touch.

Lester felt of the boot. "Woth-ferry fabric," he grunted. "It's used a lot here for making shoes and also cloaks." He turned and moved on down the path. Prechard followed. Absently, she began to pull the flowers from her hair, dropping them to the ground as she walked.

A loud guffaw greeted them from up ahead. Dennivan was standing at the edge of a line of shrubs, watching them and laughing loudly. He also wore a tunic. "Greetings, crewmates!" he waved at them.

"Greetings," Prechard waved back. "I'm glad to see that you, at least, find the clothing of this planet congenial to your tastes. The design suits you."

"Suits me?" Dennivan exploded into fresh laughter. "I sure wish I could get a look at the old man's face when he sees you! You look very beautiful, Prechard, but some people may not appreciate it." Then he pushed into the shrubs and vanished from view, leaving the other two to look after him.

Prechard shook her head. "I wonder what that was all about."

Lester shrugged. His old universe seemed very far away. As he came closer to his chambers, the beauty of Khaton was engulfing his mind through his senses, bearing significances that flowed through ancient memory and ever new discovering to surge through him in an all-pervasive wonder that would be part of him forever.

13

"Oh, no," groaned Captain Eliat. He turned away from the two who had just entered the clearing. He slid his fingers through his hair and pressed hard against his temples. Then he turned, his earlier anger spent but a new fury beginning to erupt. He forced himself to be calm enough to speak. "I have dismissed Dennivan to change his attire. He was dressed inappropriately. He is to return in uniform and with a demeanor befitting his position. And what shall I say to you?" he addressed Prechard.

"I came in haste, sir. I had not taken the time to don my uniform. I did not think you would mind."

"I do mind. Go take off the dress and put on your uniform," the Captain said wearily. He eliminated Prechard from his entire realm of awareness and looked Lester up and down. "At least you remain the same, eh, Lester? You and I and Robwill here — we have been able through our strength to maintain ourselves even though faced with a most formidable foe."

"Sir?" Lester questioned, not understanding.

"You can't imagine what has been going on here. The situation is becoming critical. You and the others have been gone for days. These women are attempting to take all of you off, to seduce you to their ways of evil and then to exterminate you. And they might well have succeeded, too, save for the fact that I am and have been aware of this little plot of theirs."

"Sir," Lester's voice was gentle, "you are very much mistaken."

"It is you who are mistaken, Lester," the Captain interrupted, "If you have allowed yourself to be taken in by these women. They are devious. I know. They will charm to their perverse way of thinking any man who is gullible in his desire to become a friend. You should have taken more care, Lester."

"This has not been my experience, sir. What prompts you to make such harsh judgment on these people?"

"I need not justify myself to you, Lester. I have observed these women. I have gone among them, and I have met extensively with their leader. I know, Lester. Have you not wondered," the Captain purred, almost crooned his question, "why you have seen no men? Or have you been more clever and fortunate than the rest of us and indeed been able to meet with your peers on this planet?"

Lester felt anger smolder in his gut. "Indeed, I have wondered," his words were clipped, "and I have discovered."

The Captain smiled magnanimously. "And what, Lester, have you discovered?"

The other man returned the smile. "I have discovered that, except for us, there are in truth no men on Khaton."

"Then where, Lester, are they?"

"They are no where, for they are not. There are no men, nor, for all intents and purposes, have there been, nor will there be."

"What?" Robwill spoke for the first time, the question exploded from him.

"Don't be a fool, Lester," said Captain Eliat coldly. "This is neither the time nor the subject for jokes."

"And I find that I have lost both the faculty and the appreciation for jokes, Captain Eliat. In fact, this is a world of women, and though they may be flesh and bone and blood, still might they not be flesh and bone and blood; for they reproduce through the grace of their sisters of the flower. They pluck their babes — all girl children, these — as fruit from the stem, and they live and grow without men, in harmony with all that is Khaton."

Captain Eliat began to pace about, muttering. "What madness is this that comes upon me masquerading as my crewman Lester? What insanity wears the guise of normalcy?" He looked at Lester with a growing terror. "Who are you behind the semblance? Get away! Cleanse yourself! Demon, leave me now and return as Lester or not at all!"

Frantically Robwill grabbed Lester by the shoulders and shoved him into the bushes. "Just wait for a little while out of his sight," he whispered urgently. "Wait until the others return, then come back. This will pass. He has been under a strain, our Captain. It will pass, and he will be himself once again. Just wait for a little while." He scurried back to where Captain Eliat stood staring glassily at the sky. "He is gone, sir," said Robwill calmly. "You can relax. Soon everything will be all right again. Can I get you some guara?"

Captain Eliat sank down onto a bench, exhausted. "Please,

Robwill, will you get me some?" He sighed audibly, then straightened his spine, pressed his shoulders back, and set his jaw. There, he waited for his crew to return to him.

14

Gently, Wyoleth guided Danal down the path, beginning the long way that would bring them to the chambers of the strangers. Arum, Allium, and Delfan followed softly behind. Wyoleth remained Sensitive, the better to guide the bent sister in her care. Still, she was surprised to feel the most tentative of approaches from Danal. Slowly, carefully, Wyoleth moved toward the feeble emanation of newly-realized being. Gently, openly, she advanced through a dark which gradually began to take on shapes and substance. A pale luminescence swelled softly to reveal a place of cool, a place of rest, of moss and quiet flowing water.

Suddenly, Wyoleth was flung back by a bolt of denial, refusal, which struck and then receded, leaving tiny jackals of rage to snap about her and at her to drive her away. Wyoleth withdrew, moved from the protecting fury which guarded a place that had appeared at first to be inviting, welcoming. From her point of being, she attempted contact with Danal. /Dear sister, I would tread gently. I do not mean to trespass. I will not again approach your mossy places or look upon these hard things of you and within you that you cover with verdant softness — moist, green places of mossy cover over stones. Do you see the stones, dear sister, or is it only others you must seek to trick?/

Stillness was complete. Wyoleth did not insist. She returned to herself, to untroubled awareness, to the younger sisters with her. They chatted. They sang. They were silent. Danal moved easily beside Wyoleth, keeping to her pace.

The approach, when it came again, was stronger, more sure, pushed forward by a strange longing kind of fear that was alien to Wyoleth.

/ . . . I . . . where do . . . you . . . take??? ?/

/We take you to the others./

/Do you bring . . . I . . . now before the women? Do you take . . . I . . . to judgment?/

/We return you to your captain and the other strangers. There has been a summons./

/ . . . I . . . do not wish to return./

Communication ended. Wyoleth was alone.

They crossed a stream and began to climb a steep hillside. "It's far to walk," Arum grumbled. "We could have flown a Photh."

"She is bent," Delfan pointed to Danal. "She cannot."

"It is far to walk," Wyoleth agreed.

"But why does she not wish to return to her sisters?" Allium's voice hung in the silence of the meadow at the top of the slope.

"This I cannot tell you," Wyoleth shrugged, "except that, perhaps, they are part of what she is bent away from."

"Then how will they be able to bring her Back?" asked Delfan.

Wyoleth shook her head. "I'm sure they have their ways — better suited to her, no doubt."

Again they were quiet.

15

Korith moved easily among the tall flowers in the Toola patch gathering the long orange seed pods. The many colors in his tunic gleamed in the light from the suns, and Korith smiled — he seemed to have discovered a taste for the gaudy among other things. He glanced down at his bare legs. The one was dark from exposure to the suns; the other was pale. He began to search for Toolas among the broad leaves, thinking of his legs: *Strange, how the fake limb is made to closely resemble the one of flesh and blood, even to the little hairs, yet no provision is made for tanning.* For the first time since his accident, he didn't mind that others should see and know.

Ganvyla worked at the other end of the patch, while Mimos and Sativa did the rows between. Dennivan would work next to him when he returned, as he had been doing before he left to answer for them both the summons of the Captain. Korith smiled. He had no doubts that the other men were experiencing wonders of self-discovery along with the feelings of peace and rightness that were part of working with their sisters of Khaton. He smiled wider, as he thought about himself and Dennivan, their own experiences, and all the changes . . . *all the changes. I was so afraid at first, he mused, and with so little reason. Indeed it is the truth that on many worlds people condemn the unknown with all the energy that they could put into learning the truth.* Again he thought of Dennivan. The thought warmed him, and he bent to his work with new energy.

Suddenly a pair of strong arms clasped him from behind and spun him around and upright. "Greetings, again." Dennivan kissed him on the lips, then released him.

"Greetings, again." Korith flushed, grinned, then looked at Dennivan, looked at the ground, looked away. "What message?"

"The Captain is strange, Korith. He will have it that you return with me immediately, and we both must wear our uniforms and be proper and play the part."

"How so, Dennivan? What is happening?"

Dennivan shrugged. "Who can say? Not I. He seemed quite mad, our Captain did. Robwill was with him being both small and consoling, but very much there to help the Captain be in charge. Captain Eliat took offense at my attire, and he ordered me away and told me in no uncertain terms to return with you immediately, us both in proper uniform and with the attitude to match." He chuckled. "As I departed, I saw Lester and Prechard approaching. Prechard was wearing a tunic gaudier than any of these, and she looked like quite the beauty." He guffawed loudly, then suddenly quieted, as he continued, "Lester was in uniform, but his eyes held a strange, alien expression; and although he appeared in semblance the same as always, his manner was not as it had been." He touched

Korith's hand and said, sober now, "We must go back and do as the Captain wishes. We are still crew, whatever else we might have become."

Korith linked his fingers through those of his friend. "Yes," he agreed, "we are crew, and crew we will be, whatever else we might remain."

16

Prechard moved swiftly over the green earth. Anger, distress, guilt, fear, and need whirled within her in cosmic chaos, nebuli of mixed emotions charting their own courses; while she sought to understand and interpret, then make meaningful, this vortex of feelings inside her.

The Captain had been insane, of that there was no doubt in Prechard's mind. Lester seemed to be possessed in some way, aloof, apart. Robwill was unobtrusive, as always. Dennivan on the path seemed the most akin to herself, but he spoke in riddles, and she did not understand him. She felt no bond with any of the crewmen. She felt no duty, and she felt no pull from any home.

So, where, now, was she bound? What, now, for herself? Prechard shook her head as if to shake off a torment of gnats. Fear and need blended into a confusion which took the shape of anger, which sapped her energy away from the Center and diffused it. The Captain had ordered her to return dressed in uniform as was a proper crew member; but Prechard did not want to be a proper crew member, nor had she ever, nor would she now.

So, what of Camas, then? Prechard would return to her, tell her what had passed between herself and the Captain, between herself and her thoughts; and Camas would listen and hear her. Surely, then, Camas would help her to sort through the turmoil, but would she? She would not tell Prechard what to do. She would not promise Prechard, nor would she be for Prechard alone. Prechard needed this of her, needed to feel the security of the only sort she was conditioned to receive; and Camas would not. What, then, for herself, Prechard? What, then, would be left to fill her, if she were to in fact turn away from her assigned future? Perhaps Camas herself was the origin and the cause of this great tumult of confusion.

Perhaps she was. And perhaps she was. She would not promise to Prechard, would not be for her alone. She had sent Prechard to the Captain, telling her to make haste, as though she knew something that Prechard did not. And she had gone, believing Camas, not questioning her. She had gone, dressed in the tunic that Camas had given her to wear, to be sent away in ridicule and disgrace, to be called beautiful as though it were the cause of great amazement.

Prechard trotted across the meadow toward the hillside, her anger growing. As she approached the place of the weavers, a small figure appeared by the trees at the top of the hill. Tiny arm went up in greeting, and the form grew larger as Camas bounded down the hill to meet Prechard coming halfway up. "Greetings again!" she cried, breathless from her run.

Prechard turned on her, hoarded confusion hurling words impatiently from her mouth — words charged with the fury that seethed among the jumble of feelings which she could not allow herself to comprehend fully, lest she be caught up in the responsibility of self-reliance and forced to make a decision. "You sent me in a skirt," she said. "You made me go there out of uniform, and I was ridiculed and ignored."

Camas pulled back, struck but not injured by this unexpected attack. "I?"

"You!" Face darkened by frowns, Prechard continued, speech pushed out of her mouth with the force of desperation. "You have confused me, and now I am unsure and uncertain."

"I?" and again, "I? Do I in truth cause your legs to move, your bladder to fill? Do I cause your brain to think, your fingers to grasp, your heart to grieve or rejoice? Come, Prechard, be reasonable."

"You! Because of you I have become perplexed, disordered, and deranged; because you have made me so!"

"No, Prechard, not because of me; for I can not, and I would not. You merely see reflected in my deeds your own desires. My words or actions may hold the image of your deepest fear or your dearest wish, but I do not rule in your life and your decisions, for such action is not possible. The ultimate source of all responsibility for all your choices and all your actions can only be yourself, your own self."

"No. You make me change. You cause me to become different. You bring into my head thoughts I do not wish to think, reveal that which I have no desire to see. Why do I question my Captain? Why, now, do I doubt my mission and my destiny?"

"The questions are yours, Prechard, to you. They must have lain long away inside you before you could confront them. Yours!"

"You make me change. I will betray my crewmates."

Camas laughed. "Change is merely movement. Why do you equate it with betrayal? And why do you place me in charge?"

"I do!" Prechard staggered away from her friend. "And what of it? What if I do?" Her voice stretched thin on the wind. "What if I do not return to my crew? What if I do not return to my mate? What, then, for me?" The force of her emotion moved her legs like pistons, carried her up the hill. Tears of frustration blinded her to all save the subtle shimmering of the place of the weavers, and her bounding steps carried her there as though it were sanctuary. "What if I do?" she shrieked down the hill. "Can I, then, replace all in my life which I would no longer have with you? Will you take me, as well, in place of all you once had? Will you give up everything for me and become my captive, filling your life with only me so that without me you will have nothing? Will you become the reality of my fantasy of possession and security? Will you keep me in my dream? Will you?"

She bolted in among the exquisite latticework of hanging fabrics to chambers draped with webs, nests, and hammocks, all blending with a harmony of perfection into the total pattern. She whirled about, her struggling senses overwhelmed by the crashing multitude of fibers that were woven into tapestries of many hues, opaque, transparent, opalescent, sparkling, bold and varied, each point of meaning drawn forth by the weaver through both thread and pattern into a great craft of creation. Prechard spun about, seeking without reason or direction, wide-eyed and wild. "Mine!" she cried.

"She will not be mine, to me!" She stumbled against a woody knee, caught at a thick, brocaded drapery. "So what shall I have then?" With a painful rending, the drapery separated from the wooden frame which held it, tore apart and fell, wrapping Prechard in its heavy folds, as it bore her to the ground.

Anthemis, eldest of the weavers, bent over Prechard. Her wide blue eyes peered over the high bridge of her generous nose. Her hair hung to her shoulders in thick locks of yellow and white. She gestured to Prechard as she spoke, long, graceful fingers fanning from outstretched hands. "What passes with you, strange sister? What passes?" Her voice was soft, her tone soothing.

Prechard blinked, as the face of Anthemis blurred and receded in her vision. "She will not be other than who she is," she croaked. "She will only be herself. She will not be my fantasy. She will likewise leave me to myself, to be only me, and will demand no changes from me. So where, then, old one, lies the contest?"

"There is no contest."

"Where, in that case, is the reason for struggle?"

"There is no reason for struggle."

"Where, then, the conflict?" Prechard's voice rose, shrill, demanding.

Anthemis remained calm. "There is no conflict."

"How can that be? How can such a thing be?" Prechard swallowed herself, choked, and washed herself down with anguish to wallow in the farthest depths of her soul to seek the answer.

From far off sounded the whisper of Anthemis, accents swirling through Prechard's sphere of sounds, "You must face and master that within yourself which keeps you from being whole. Therein lies the only contest, and this will be your survival and your salvation."

17

Korith and Dennivan sat apart in the clearing near their chambers. Their bent knees and the angles of their fingers as they clutched their cups of steaming guara pointed to one another, and their bent heads inclined in each other's direction. Lester sat alone, apart from all the others, staring at the mist which rose from his own hot beverage, while Robwill kept anxious eyes focused on the captain who paced back and forth, muttering to himself, exploding every now and then into short sentences directed at any or all of the men or no one in particular. "Where is Prechard all this time?" he grumbled, "and where is Danal at all?" He spun about and faced Robwill. "It must be part of their Plan to keep us separated, to allow some of us to meet together but not all of us, the better to rule us through anxiety, eh, Robwill?"

"I couldn't say, sir," Robwill attempted to console the Captain. "Perhaps they are both on their way here and will arrive shortly."

Captain Eliat paced. He marched in a circle, then over to Lester. "Perhaps Time will soon clarify for you the Truth behind these Actions which you seem to have mistaken for Kindness from these women." Lester continued to gaze at the steam from his guara. Korith and Dennivan glanced at one another, then away. The Captain strode over to stand before them. "And you? Can it be true that you also have been seduced to a state of Unreason? Have you not wondered about the absence of our Kind? Have you no concern that our fate may be the same as that of the other unwilling males — to satisfy these evil spiders, and then, drained of our vitality, be trashed and done away with?"

"I would like to speak," drawled Lester from where he sat, "in my turn and as is our own custom. I would like to tell a bit of history that you all might find to be interesting enough: Once there were men on Khaton, but not for long. Now there are no men; nor have there been for countless seasons." Briefly, Lester gave an accounting, a description of his experience with the Hylantree, but only his experiences of the past. He did not speak of things which would cause the others to wonder in any way what he had become in the process. He told the story as he had experienced it, and when he reached the conclusion, he was finished, and he stopped speaking.

Captain Eliat had seated himself on a stump while Lester was talking. Now he rose to his feet, seeming to stand forever, stretching miles into the air. "That is nonsense!" he proclaimed. "This entire story is obviously a fiction, a myth, a tale devised to keep you from discovering the truth about this world. Nonsense. I am surprised at you, Lester, for allowing yourself to be taken in this manner."

Lester snorted. "You say 'nonsense'," he confronted the Captain, "and 'nonsense' because I offer an explanation which leaves you out. There is neither need nor place for us, for you or for me, Captain Eliat, not even for you or for me, in this world. We are not necessary in any way whatsoever to the life scheme of this planet. This is a fact, although it is difficult to accept — especially by you, Captain Eliat. It is much simpler to say 'nonsense' and let it go at that."

Captain Eliat clucked softly. "You are gullible, Lester. You have been taken in. I should have thought that you, of all men, would have been stronger." He turned his back on Lester and addressed Dennivan. "And what about you? You who came back in a Dress — what have YOU to tell us?"

"Indeed we have seen more than what we are familiar with," Dennivan said softly. "The women have been . . . have been . . . ah, but what can I say that will tell it all? And I in turn have become . . . have become . . . well, I have become . . ."

"You sound like a three-copper operetta," the Captain sneered. "Not a word of those which tumble forth through your flabby mouth makes sense. What have you become, become, become, Dennivan, that you defend these predatory females with more nonsense than that which Lester spewed? Have they taken your brain and sent me back only the husk of my crewman?"

"I remain crewman," Dennivan's voice was level, "whatever else I might have become, and I will have the respect due me by my Captain."

Captain Eliat turned his back on Dennivan. "Dare I try to hear what you may have to say, Korith?" he asked. "Dare I risk another rude awakening, another exposure to the loss of all reason among my once strong crewmen? Have they gotten to you, as well, Korith? Have you, also, been taken?"

Korith gulped. He stared not at the Captain but at a point behind him, over his shoulder. The Captain turned, and the other men followed with their gazes.

Wyoleth had entered the clearing. She stood quietly, Arum and Allium on her left. On her right was a creature and then a girl who was strange to the men . . . a creature between the woman and the girl . . . a creature with hollow, bleeding eyes that stared separately at visions of their own, visions of hell from the soul of torment. Foam and mucous dripped from his slack, wet mouth and dried into his beard, while his tangled hair stood out as though trying to free itself from his scalp and fly far from the terror inside the skull where set its roots.

The other men recoiled. Then Captain Eliat took a step toward Danal, then a step back, another step forward and then back again. Hesitating for long moments, he appeared to rock back and forth in a strange dance of confront and deny. Then he broke into his approach, nearly surged forward at the woman. "What have you done to him?" he croaked.

Wyoleth replied simply, with fact, seeming not to be disturbed by the reaction of the men. "We brought her to your summons. She is bent. She could not come alone. Delfan found her, and she was bent. We had formed a net and were attempting to lead her back to the present of no threat, but the summons came, and we we brought her here to answer."

"What do you mean . . . *bent*?" roared the Captain, all control gone. "What do you mean . . . *her*? Get away from *him*! What have you done to *him*?"

Wyoleth backed away, motioning for the girls to follow. They looked about the circle of faces, seeing mirrored there the shock which the Captain used to hurl hatred at them. Time appeared to halt for all save the four of them. They flowed over the ground toward the woods, and the men watched them, stared, gripped by the appearance of Danal, until the women melted into the brush and vanished from sight.

"Go after them!" the Captain shrieked at his men. "Get them!" No one moved. "Will you let them escape?" the Captain closed his eyes and breathed deeply, a storm rattling in his chest. Then he opened his eyes too wide and approached Lester. "So," he smiled with his lips, an ugly grin, "do you still insist that your friends mean us no harm? Look what they have done." He moaned, a long, low sound filled with pain and desperation. "Alas, poor Danal, what shall we do? How can we restore you?" He whirled about, fumbling at his belt. "They must have gone for the others. We will be in mortal danger with every passing moment. We must prepare for our last defense." He walked slowly to where Danal stood. Weeping, he took one limp hand in both his own and stroked the torn skin. "I have called down the globe."

18

Prechard writhed among folds of fabric, seeking to release herself from her fear which thwarted the possibilities of her future. Camas remained, and indeed there was no conflict save that which raged within herself, to and of and from and by and for her alone. Camas remained, and she, Prechard, what would she do? Where was she at? What would there be for her, she who had always done her best to step away from any contest requiring confrontation? Prechard wrestled with the drapery, seeking to resolve her question, searching for an answer as though it lay hidden among the pleats of material; until, with a sudden wink of time, she was not . . .

. . . Far from the world of her senses, Prechard hung suspended, until dream materialized as form, and her feet in dream thudded against the ground . . .

Prechard felt gentle air caress her naked skin, watched as it rippled soft dunes of blue desert sand. Blue shining like the finest of sapphires rose gleaming peaks of ridges in the distance running across the horizon. Sand under her bare soles was warm, easy to her feet, and she moved freely over the desert ground with no need to search for a path. The ridges waited.

Prechard moved forward through time and space, moving forward over the sands of the desert, moving forward across blue sand toward the ridges. One foot leading the other, Prechard moved over blue desert sand gentle beneath her feet, giving easily to her step and never hindering her, never dragging nor abrasive, never dusty nor treacherous. Always moving forward, there was no longer time nor space but only the journey. *The ridges remained, as Prechard was, as were the blue sands of the desert; and Prechard moved forward.*

Prechard stood at the foot of the ridges. Blue sand led up to sheer rock wall, no plain or boulders or foothills for transition. She ran her hands over the smooth face before her. Shining blue, deep gleaming from within sending stars of brightness to break in light from the surface of the stone, the flat ridge wall rose sleek and abrupt from the warm sand.

Placing palm and fingertips against the smooth blue stone, Prechard began to climb. Up the polished surface she went, ascending, rising over the desert. Pressing hands and toes against the rock, she mounted ever upward. *The ridge peaks tower somewhere far above, and the rock wall is, and the climbing.*

Prechard reached the ceiling—slight curve of blue dome reaching around as far as she could see, sealing her in a globe, a bubble of cerulean light. Floor and wall and roof became the same, and Prechard moved forward over the gently sloping surface.

Prechard moved forward until she came to the crack. Pressing her face against the tiny fissure, she peered within, seeing. Then, pushing slightly, she entered the crack; and leaving all azure behind, she came into the garden.

And there in the center of the garden was Blossom.

Prechard approached Blossom and bent close. Blossom reached out to envelop her. She felt the soft coolness of velvet petals surround her face and stroke her hot skin, bathing her in a glory of sweet-scented balm, refreshing her. Blossom sang to her, called her to come; and joyfully she went. Professing beauty in promise all the while, she lured Prechard down into the depths of her soul where, in all trust and grati-tude, she released herself and became Blossom.

Being Blossom, again she watched Prechard approach, bend close. Speaking softly, she drew her in, all identity fad-ing to a fleeting transparency. Gleefully, she allowed herself to be led. Enraptured by the wonder of Blossom, she swept herself away in a whirlpool pattern of petals. Drowning in the dear perfume, she glided among Blossom through her ever descending rows of mazes of labyrinths of on and down ap-proaching at last the Center where waited all Light and Dark and Glory—AND THERE STOOD ONLY A HUGE AND BRISTLY UGLY BUG!

Oh, deep and evil soul of Blossom!

Rank and dank and putrid Center!

Lie and falsehood and untruth!

Betrayal!

Fear!

Anger!

A sharp chord sounded, and Prechard faced the bug in the Center of Blossom. Vibrations quivered the air, and bug stood, obvious, apparent, there. But wait! Prechard shook her head and blinked her eyes. Something was not Right about bug. There seemed to be no real movement, no defini-tion. Why, could it be??? Yes, there was no bug at all; no bug but only a shadow—a deep and brilliant shadow cast by her own image as she stood before the Light!

(a deep and brilliant shadow cast by her own image as she stood before the Light)

Laughing, she waved her arms, and the shadow mirrored the movement. She chuckled with the glee of her discovery. There, in the heart of Blossom, experience could only be a reminiscence upon return.

So did Prechard come back from Blossom. She withdrew from among singing petals, psalms glorifying the passage and the progress. Cool flesh of flower walls eased her going, per-mitting her to separate while still granting her company.

Blossom Beautiful!

Prechard was, again. Moving easily, now, she freed herself from the encumbering drapery, rose, and strode from the chambers of the weavers.

19

Danal had been bathed, shaved, and dressed in a clean medical smock, but he looked little better than before. He sat and drooled, while Captain Eliat stormed and pleaded, cajoled and threatened, ordered Danal to return to awareness and promised him a thousand rewards if he would. Danal remained away. He complied when physically moved in any direction. Other than that, he displayed no sign at all that his body was inhabited.

At last, Captain Eliat guided his crewman to the infirmary and laid him on a medical couch. As he began inserting into Danal's veins the needles which would sustain his life, he moaned aloud, "Ah, Danal, how I wish that I could take your pain unto myself and bear it for you!" Tears flowed down his cheeks and splashed onto Danal's smock. Captain Eliat unwound a set of wires and plastic hookups which were connected to the wall console which, in turn, was connected directly to the great computer that ran the globe. "Have no fear," the Captain patted Danal's hand, then began to connect the colored wires to the other man's head, body and limbs, "we shall escape this demon planet. I, your Captain, promise you this. We shall take you Home and find a Cure for this monstrous condition, induced, no doubt, by these devil women." He completed the wiring operation and stepped to the keyboard of the console. He pressed several buttons, and a low hum began. "There." He stepped back and rubbed his hands together with satisfaction, while the machine began the long process of analysis procedure that would eventually lead to a diagnosis which would then be followed by the treatment of Danal.

Captain Eliat left the infirmary and shut the door firmly behind him. In the long corridor, Korith and Dennivan sorted and stacked boxes of specimens that Lester was carrying up the ramp and loading just inside the doorway. They looked at the Captain as he hurried past, eyes set straight ahead, and decided not to speak to him.

Captain Eliat entered the control room where Robwill sat monitoring the view screens. Images of the landscape surrounding the globe showed stillness and peace. "Everything's fine, sir," Robwill said.

"You don't know that!" Captain Eliat turned on the younger man, snapping, snarling. "You can't say that for certain! Believe me, Robwill," he leaned toward the other, "I Know. All and Everything on this accursed planet appears harmless, gives an impression of being benign, nay, even benevolent. But it is Not, Robwill. It is Not. This planet is by far the most dangerous of all the worlds we have yet explored, for here threat appears as no threat at all. My men have been bemused and spellbound. All, Robwill, except for myself and possibly you, although I could not say for certain about you — all have been entrapped, ensorcelled, and removed of their wits by these savage females. It is only because of the Great Strength and Diplomacy which I used to master their ruler that my men have been returned to me, and each has been damaged in some way. And Danal," the Captain sobbed harshly, "Danal has been robbed of his very Self; and how shall we restore him?" He spun around, as one of the small screens at the far end of the room began to sputter. Robwill leaped from his seat and ran to the communication controls. He twisted a dial and pressed a series of buttons beneath the screen, and the unexpected image of Prechard came into focus. She still wore her tunic, and although she appeared tired and rumpled, she spoke through lips curved into a great smile:

". . . on, so I know you are receiving me. And, as whoever is there will have no problem in determining, I am not hooked up to receive any broadcast from you — and that is exactly the way I intend for the situation to remain. As my final act of responsibility to Captain and Crew, I shall formally inform you of my decision."

Captain Eliat grabbed at the panel, leaned on all of the communications buttons. "Prechard!" he roared, "Take off that skirt and get back here! We're ready to leave! Get back here right away!"

". . . the time it takes." Prechard had been speaking. "It was a simple matter to set everything up, and as soon as my message is complete, I shall destroy my uniform and eliminate all traces."

"Prechard," commanded Captain Eliat coldly, "I order you to return here immediately. Return here or be subject to a Hearing and Decision Process."

Prechard continued, "I wish only for the message which I will transmit to be truly and duly recorded, and then I shall be free. Captain Eliat!" The Captain jerked at the mention of his name. "I withdraw my service. I formally withdraw. I withdraw without regret. I will rid myself of all articles of duty. I shall no longer be Crew member. I will remain here in a secret place where no one will ever be able to find me, so do not bother to try. I will stay here and be free, myself, my very own." The screen went dark. The image was gone.

"Then stay," Captain Eliat snapped at the dark glass, his shoulders heaving, "fool!"

Robwill was frantically flipping switches. He held one side of a set of headphones against his ear. His eyes were wide and frightened. He turned to the Captain. "I can't find her, sir," he said anxiously. "I am trying in every way I know how, but I can't seem to get any location for her."

Captain Eliat laughed, a short, nasty sound. "Then let her stay here. We will leave without her."

Robwill stared at him. "But, sir, we can't do that. We can't go off and leave her here. We can't abandon a crewmate."

"Oh yes we can, Robwill. We can, and we can, and we will. Let her stay. She has been insubordinate. She will be under arrest. She can just stay here. We will go without her." The Captain turned and strode from the room. "Prepare to lift the globe at the end of the quarter," he called back.

20

The bulk of the great globe almost filled the clearing. The men had loaded all their gear, and they were ready to go. The men waited. Danal, wired and plugged to the great computer, waited and was not. Robwill waited in the control room, frantically, hastily, and without orders, searching for some trace somewhere of Prechard. Korith and Dennivan waited in the Crew Lounge, alone, seated in separate chairs as close to one another as they dared. Neither spoke, but from time to time their eyes met, softened, and their lips curved in memory and with promise.

Lester lay on his back on the pallet in his old chamber, eyes closed, body completely still. He had come again down the ramp to bring in the last of the parcels, and while he was still in the clearing, he felt a call, a compulsion. He surrendered immediately, eagerly, almost greedily, following the force which pulled him to his chamber, led him inside, pressed him to recline, relax, release. Memory propelled him, helped him to hurtle himself from himself and away, out and free then, free to ride the winds of the cosmos, free to breathe free, not-being, all: *Laugh, shout forth joy and jubilation — not-being, formless, bliss. Lift swiftly, soar, fly freely, without shape or substance, Laughter resounding, roar of free spirit supreme hurling echoes through endless depths of cosmos sounds down through fathoms of the universe, joy and jubilation, bliss absolute.*

Captain Eliat strode down the long ramp, boots striking sound to ring from the hard surface. "Lester," he called, "let's go. What's keeping you?"

Lester came out from his chamber. "Captain," he said, "go without me. I wish to remain on Khaton. Go on, and leave me here."

Captain Eliat's face sagged, losing all form in an elasticity of surprise and shock. His eyes bulged, then retreated far into the sockets, as his cheeks and forehead pressed around them in a squint of confusion and denial. A strange, twisted noise issued from his mouth, pressing his lips into a grotesque shape. Then all wrinkles and creases smoothed away into a blank expanse of skin, and the Captain blinked. "Ah, Lester," he crooned, lips smiling tenderly, sympathetically, "you have been misled. Fear not, nor do you worry, for I shall take it upon myself to protect you and to lead you away from this overwhelming threat. I will not allow the evil of this world to so spirit you away. I will help you, my poor, twisted friend and crewman." He took the other man's hands gently in his own. "Lester," he looked directly into his face, "you must not be well. You need to be healed. Why, you yourself told me that no man can hope to remain here and live. You told me so. You did. And that men are neither needed nor wanted here. You said so. How, then, can you even consider staying? Poor Lester. Come with me now to our globe, and all together we will leave this accursed planet."

Lester pulled out of the Captain's grasp but did not move away. Steadily, he leaned his will against the being of the other man, seeking a core which he had long been turned away from. "I wish to remain, sir," he repeated, "and remain on Khaton is exactly what I intend to do."

Captain Eliat responded, but not quite as Lester had expected. He pressed his great sorrow against Lester, attempting to bear him down with dependency and guilt. "Consider, Lester," he reasoned, "the tragedy, the death that awaits you. Consider myself, then, and the other men, your crew brothers. Consider how we would feel if we were to actually leave you here." He pressed his palm to his chest and bowed his head forward as though in great pain. "How," his voice quavered, "could we possibly live with our guilt and shame if we permitted you to remain to your death?"

"Death carries new meaning for me now, since I have realized that I have first to learn what is life. I will remain." Lester bore this desire down upon the unconscious will of the Captain, seeking to impress upon the other man the need for him to do this thing.

Captain Eliat grew stern. "Well, I simply cannot permit you to do this foolish thing, Lester." He spoke paternally, expecting obedience. "You may not, of course, remain here on Khaton. You will, of course, board the globe and come away with us. Now, turn you right around, Lester, and step, step, step to it."

Lester smiled at the Captain. Then he played his final card—one he had not until then even known he carried—sending it spinning into the game with a flip, his strength swirling through orders from his Captain, his will expanding to control his own fate. With no further thought, Lester gave himself up and plunged into the spiritual labyrinth that belonged to the Captain in an attempt to flow through and out the other side.

Thus began his soul's journey through those twisted corridors, through chambers of corruption where sounded constant banshee wailing; demons of despair sobbing and weeping through the obscurity of indefinite dreams.

There was no place for joy here. No place for beauty.

The corridor opened into a cavern thickly hung with webs which dusted the air with perpetual motes of filth that fell from the fangs of the webs' denizens; and there, on a stool of rusted metal, crouched the squat form which enshrouded the essence of the Captain that Lester was to face and to triumph over.

REPULSE

REPEL

Lester stopped.

REVULSION

REPULSION

DISGUST

DECAY

NAUSEA

Mouth (a slit across the entire thick section where tiny, pointed head merged with compressed, warty body) drooled and drizzled. Round eyes set to each side of this gash stared at Lester, lidded over every now and again with a viscous yellow curtain. Then, with a rending, sucking noise, the huge maw opened, and a tongue, slick with putrescent mucous, flicked out and wrapped around Lester at the middle of his body. Wrenching him about, it drew him swiftly into mouth, down throat, and through gullet, loosing him to splash into a pool of pulpy liquid.

Spongy hunks of decomposed stuff clung to Lester's hair and face, and he gagged at the stench of it. Drawing all his will and strength to his command, he plunged beneath the warm, murky fluid, down and deep, down to the very bottom where a sudden current caught him and rushed him into and along a passage. So he traveled, until time and space lost all meaning, and finally, crowded among putrid lumps, he came once again into the world beyond; and when he stood on his own feet and looked around, he found that he was in the clearing among the empty chambers of the men. Beyond him stood Captain Eliat, and behind the Captain waited the great globe. Lester stared at them, and he realized that he had mastered his fear and uncertainty. Ahead was only Khaton, all Life Everlasting,; ahead was only Khaton, all Death Absolute.

"Well, Lester," urged the Captain, "move on, on, on. Let's go, please. Everyone is waiting for you."

Lester knew that now he could use illusion to save himself. He placed before the Captain a fabrication to cover his departure. Then he turned, his presence spreading through the air like mist, hovering over the ground, drifting toward underbrush to vanish in the woods.

Captain Eliat smiled and nodded his head. "Good, Lester." He watched the form before him move to the globe. "I knew you would be reasonable. Now, up you go." He gestured, hesitated for a moment, then strode up the ramp, last to enter as was proper for a Captain. The great door slid closed, and the Lycoperdon lifted into space.

NIGHTHAWK

by

Artemis OakGrove

$8.95

The latest from the dripping hot pen of Artemis OakGrove takes you to the underground world of the city ghetto where turf is controlled by fierce strength and cunning. Lori, unsuspecting, enters this world dominated by the warlord Nighthawk. Claimed, chained and branded by 'Hawk, Lori becomes the property of the subway Club.

Her struggle to maintain an identity, and 'Hawk's to keep control of her turf and her gangs, is interwoven with raw sex and sensitivity, dominance and dependency. It's another world out there—on Nighthawk's turf.

THE RAGING PEACE
Volume One of the Throne Trilogy

by

Artemis OakGrove

$7.95

Meet Ryan, millionare butch who flies her own plane, rides a motorcycle and wears leather. She meets and pursues Leslie, an attorney who has everything one wants in a femme—beauty, brains and passion. The surrounding cast of bitchy femmes, dominating dykes, sex slaves and naive high school girls are all being manipulated by the deadly Anara—from another world 3000 years past

DREAMS OF VENGEANCE
Volume Two of the Throne Trilogy

by

Artemis OakGrove

$7.95

Continuing the sage of the luxury of a shared life—Ryan and Leslie, attended by their sex slaves Sanji and Corelle—a life filled with excesses from sex to sumptious living. But in the background lurks the demi-goddess Anara, bent on revenge against the members of her clan who where responsible for her death 3000 years before.

THRONE OF COUNCIL
Volume Three of the Throne Trilogy
by
Artemis OakGrove
$7.95

The spell-binding conclusion of the Throne Trilogy. Anara plans to deliver the final blow to Ryan, her only contender for the coveted role of Queen Regent of the Throne of Council. But even she doesn't know the true identity of the reigning Queen Regent who is determined to stop her and pass the succession on to Ryan who would rule the spirit world with love and compassion for milleniums – or until another such as Anara lusts for power and dominance . . .

TRAVELS WITH DIANA HUNTER
by
Regine Sands
$8.95

"From the first innocent nuzzle at the 'neck of nirvana' to the final orgasmic fulfillment, Regine Sands stirs us with her verbal foreplay, tongue in cheek humor and tongue in many other places eroticism."

— Jewelle Gomez

When sixteen-year-old diana Hunter and Christine Tyler run away from Lubbock, Texas together it is the beginning of an odyssey that spans almost two decades of togetherness and separation. And in that separation, Diana must deal with a veritable parade of women attracted by her brilliance, her wit, but most of all – her body.

JOURNEY TO ZELINDAR
by
Diana Rivers
$9.95

Lace's first Lesbian adventure fantasy " . . . follows Sair as she flees the male enclave of Eezore and crosses the Red Line which marks the boundary of the Hadra dominions. What she discovers is a society of adventurous women, where Lesbianism is the norm and psychic rather than physical weapons are used in war. Rivers has done an incredible job in creating her world, which unfolds before us in all of its wonders and with a wealth of detail."

— *The Weekly News*

A THIRD STORY
by
Carole Taylor
$7.95

At a time when many gays would retreat to the closet and lock the door behind them, here is a novel that tells how women from three generations deal with coming out in a college community. When one woman decides to fight the battle of salary equity, a threat of exposure is used to silence her. With her lover, a lawyer, she decides to fight back in court. Her action touches students and staff members as they deal with the color lavender.

Ms. Taylor tells the tale with all the wit and wisdom of *Up the Down Staircase.* You'll find someone you know — or would like to-on every page. And, Ms. Taylor is donating 10% of her profits to AIDS research and to benefit AIDS patients.

JUST HOLD ME
by
Linda Parks
$7.95

Why has Constance Brooks been sentenced to prison for a crime she did not commit? Her lover's mother, the residents and the criminal justice system of a small midwest community don't really care. She isn't the kind of woman they understand or even want to try. From prison, Constance tries to prove she did not kill her lover. Discover how the American justice system works — or doesn't work — and how women forced to live subject to it find ways to cope and survive.

THE LEADING EDGE
An Anthology of Lesbian Sexual Fiction
Introduction by Pat Califia
$9.95

A number 1 best seller, already in its third printing! This hottest, sexiest collection of Lesbian erotica includes an introduction *The Edge of Cunt* by Pat Califia that is worth the price of the book. Included are selections from Ann Allen Shockley, Dorothy Allison, Jewelle

Gomez, Merril Mushroom, Artemis Oakgrove and other storytellers of real life and fantasy erotica.

Meet Cass, the highway patrolwoman, who apprehends a blonde speed demon . . . Miss Todd, who looks so very handsome in her riding togs . . . Carol and Liz who drive around the country in their van looking for women . . . a gang of female buccaneers who take command of the Gulf Coast . . . and the plantation mistress and the slave girl.

ORDER TODAY (clip or photocopy this coupon)

_____	copies	The Raging Peace	00-1	$7.95 ea. =	_____
_____	copies	Dreams of Vengeance	05-2	$7.95 ea. =	_____
_____	copies	Throne of Council	08-7	$7.95 ea. =	_____
_____	copies	A Third Story	06-0	$7.95 ea. =	_____
_____	copies	Travels with Diana Hunter	07-9	$8.95 ea. =	_____
_____	copies	Just Hold Me	02-8	$7.95 ea. =	_____
_____	copies	The Leading Edge	09-5	$9.95 ea. =	_____
_____	copies	Journey to Zelindar	10-9	$9.95 ea. =	_____
_____	copies	Nighthawk	11-7	$8.95 ea. =	_____
		Colorado residents please add 3.6% tax		=	_____
		Postage/handling in US & Canada		$1.50 =	1.50
		Total in US funds		=	_____

_____ enclosed check or money order

_____ charge my MasterCard/VISA   account #   _____

expiration date _____   signature   _____

Name _____

Address _____

City _____ State _____ Zip _____

Send order form and payment to: Lace Publications, PO Box 10037, Denver, CO 80210-0037 USA

THANK YOU.